Dedication

This story is dedicated in memory of my grandfather, William 'Duke' Procter (August 18, 1899 — December 14, 2005), who set foot in three centuries, went skydiving in celebration of his 100th birthday, was the oldest competing horseshoe player in Canada for several years, square-danced until 103, took up five-pin bowling at 92 (still getting strikes at 104!), and could whack a snake to pieces with the best of them before finally expiring at 106 as the last surviving British Columbian to have served his country in The Great War.

Duke's vitality and spirit never failed to inspire me. Rest in peace, Grampa. You deserve it.

BORROWING ALEX

Nikki wants to get married more than anything. But what's she to do when her fiancé Royce is dragging his heels over setting a date? Why, fake a fling with the best man, of course! Ambushing Alex may be a tad desperate, but pretending she's hot for him just might kick-start Royce's attention . . . Alex is definitely not on board with this plan. But he quickly realizes Nikki isn't a wild party girl at all. She's cute, sweet — and faithful. Against his common sense, he's falling for her . . .

CINDY PROCTER-KING

BORROWING ALEX

Complete and Unabridged

LINFORD
Leicester

First published in Great Britain in 2013

First Linford Edition
published 2015

A catalogue record for this book is available
from the British Library.

ISBN 978–1–4448–2336–3

Published by
F. A. Thorpe (Publishing)
Anstey, Leicestershire

Set by Words & Graphics Ltd.
Anstey, Leicestershire
Printed and bound in Great Britain by
T. J. International Ltd., Padstow, Cornwall

This book is printed on acid-free paper

1

Here Goes Something

Nikki St. James was no criminal. Merely desperate.

And desperate times called for desperate measures.

In her cramped hiding place behind the massive rhododendron bush, Nikki pushed a cluster of white blossoms out of her face. The shingles siding the old Seattle house scratched her back through her turtleneck. Matching rhododendron-green yoga pants and black ankle boots completed her camouflage ensemble.

Normally, she would never wear such a dark shade of green.

Signaling her cousin, Karin Russell, to follow her lead, Nikki tugged on a makeshift pantyhose mask. *Ouch, that hurts*.

The tight nylon yanked her short curls,

but it couldn't be helped. The beige mesh screening her vision squashed a blonde lock into one eye. Her breath whistled through her nostrils while her heart raced faster than a frightened rabbit's.

Yep, on a scale of one to ten, Nikki estimated her current desperation level ran at an all-time 9.99 high. Nerves and excitement scrambled to catch up.

All things come to those who take action. Or something like that.

Spitting out a speck of pantyhose lint, Nikki turned to help Karin tuck her loose brown waves beneath an identical mask. The remaining length of hose dangled off Karin's head like a mutated ponytail. Nikki's cousin looked ridiculous.

Wait a minute. Did she?

Whatever. Time was running short. Nikki only hoped that, for Alex Hart, the element of surprise when they ambushed him catapulted 'ridiculous' into the category of something more like 'menacing.'

'Here,' she whispered, retrieving a coiled rope from the supplies on the ground and passing the loop to Karin. 'The duct tape can wait until you tie his hands,' she instructed. She reached for the black pillowcase and child's toy space gun purchased a few days ago. The rhododendron leaves rustled against her legs in the late-afternoon breeze of mid-May. 'If we work fast enough, we'll have him in the van in under two minutes.'

Karin winced. 'Nikki, are you sure about this? Kidnapping Royce's best man seems a bit drastic.'

'Karin, we've talked until I'm green in the face,' Nikki whispered. 'Don't you think I feel bad enough about . . . borrowing Alex already?'

'Then why not explain to him — ?'

'I can't. He'll think I'm nuts. He'll never agree to help me unless he feels he has no choice.'

'You don't know that.'

'Yes, I do.' Nikki had been acquainted with Alex Hart, her fiancé's intended

3

best man, for over two years. They'd met at the society engagement party her parents had hosted soon after Royce Carmichael had proposed.

However, 'acquainted' was the operative word. Nikki didn't know Alex well enough to saunter over to the intelligent history professor and casually ask his cooperation in her last-ditch effort to boot Royce into action. Although the two men had remained friends since rooming together as college freshmen, they rarely socialized. Nikki knew *about* Alex, but she could count on the fingers of one hand the occasions during which she'd actually talked to the guy.

Royce had explained the situation once. Between his busy schedule as an associate in her father's dermatology practice and Alex's determination to fast-track his way to tenure at prestigious Pacific University, neither man possessed the luxury to coddle their relationship.

Nikki couldn't fathom sharing a similar fate with Karin. At twenty-five, she might be six years younger than Royce and his pal, but she valued friendship. She and Karin had been BFFs since childhood. In fact, they were closer than Nikki and her older sister — her parents' favorite.

She puffed out a breath. 'You're right, kidnapping Alex Hart could be considered drastic. But, Karin, that's the point.' Nikki's nose itched beneath the stretched nylon. She scratched her squished nostril, and her huge diamond solitaire engagement ring glittered in the shadows of the giant rhododendron.

'Kidnapping — I mean, borrowing — Alex is the only way I can think of to get through to Royce. Talking has accomplished squat.' The nylon pressed her lashes into her eyes like tiny, spiky instruments of torture. Biting her lip, she glanced at her watch. According to her legwork, Alex Hart would arrive home any minute. 'Besides, it was your brainwave that I make Royce jealous by pretending I'm attracted to another guy. That I might even sleep with him.

If we dismiss the borrowing aspect, that's really all I'm doing.'

Karin's face paled beneath her pantyhose mask. 'Nikki, that was a joke! I didn't for one second believe you'd try to make Royce jealous by *borrowing* a guy from your wedding party.'

Nikki's stomach knotted. 'It *has* to be Alex,' she half-whispered. 'Royce knows all my male friends, and he doesn't feel threatened by a single one. No, pretending I've fallen for a friend of his — and not just any friend, but his best man — will prove how intolerable our situation has become. Karin, I can't stand this forever-a-fiancée waiting. With Royce dragging his heels about us setting the date, I'm starting to believe there'll never *be* a wedding, unless I do something about it. And Mother and Father seem to think *I'm* stalling.'

'I know, and that's awful. But — '

'No buts.' Nikki parted the waxy bush leaves, and a cluster of blossoms riffled. She scanned the parking area several yards behind the house. *Empty.*

She looked back at Karin. 'If Royce still wants to marry me like he says, then it's time for him to ante up. If he loves me, he'll take this fake booty call I've engineered with Alex as serious indication that he'd better make an honest woman out of me fast.' Clutching the pillowcase, she pointed a finger skyward. 'Nikki St. James is nobody's fool.'

Okay, she had her doubts about that last statement. Maybe Royce *was* playing her for a fool. Maybe he no longer wanted to get married, but didn't know how to tell her.

Tears pricked her eyes. She blinked them away. *Think positive.*

Royce was busy, that was all. Too harried to notice the flying tendency of time. Well, after the surprise she'd arranged for later tonight, he'd have to be thicker than the bricks in the little pig's house *not* to take action.

Her hopes rode on that risk. Her future happiness depended on Royce's reaction to the note she'd left on her kitchen table.

The puttering of a car in the alley announced Alex Hart's arrival. Holding her breath, Nikki peeked through the bush again.

A classic Volkswagen Beetle pulled into the gravel parking area. As Alex Hart stepped out of the small yellow car, the sun, filtering through the gray Seattle sky, glinted off his neatly trimmed, nutmeg-brown hair.

Luckily, he hadn't noticed her van parked in the alley. Or, at least, he hadn't questioned the presence of the old vehicle.

Good, stashing the van down the road multiple times over the last week had worked.

She wanted him unprepared and completely unsuspecting.

'He's here,' she whispered to Karin. 'No more discussion. It's too late to jam out.' Her heart jack-hammered against her ribs. She tightened her grip on the toy gun. 'Get ready to jump him.'

Alex Hart wanted to vegetate. To collapse on the couch and indulge in a mind-numbing action movie while consuming mass quantities of pizza and chugging an ice-cold beer. Then sack out in front of the blaring TV with his feet sticking off the sofa — and his socks on.

To speak to no one. And not move a muscle.

To sleep the sleep of the happy dead until morning.

To take a break from playing the infested-with-departmental-politics, ivory-tower game.

Loafers crunching gravel, Alex locked his restored 1976 Super Beetle. He placed his laptop case on the hood and tugged off the glasses he wore for driving or lecturing when he felt bagged like this. He rubbed his gritty eyes.

The fatigue he swore had replaced his bone marrow during this last semester dug within him, and he pushed out a sigh. Making like a sloth over the next week would provide a welcome contrast from the hectic pace of supervising exams, attending commencement as an assistant history professor, and, this afternoon, finalizing grades on the student web portal and catering to the dean's ego. The latter was a necessary evil of pursuing tenure that Alex abhorred.

Idiot box, here I come. He couldn't wait.

There was nothing like the flash of ammunition jolting off a big screen to rejuvenate a guy. With a deadline to an academic journal looming, Alex craved relaxation. In five short weeks the second summer session would begin. He needed to prep materials for his American History seminar, which allowed him seven blissful days of slacking off, although his mind and body begged for more.

Much more.

Unfortunately, assistant professors didn't earn nearly enough cash to justify a quick island-paradise jaunt. He'd have to content himself with bursts of sunshine between Washington's spring rains.

He slipped his glasses into his laptop case. Ruminating over the pizza delivery menu taped to the fridge, he flipped through his bulky keychain and ambled toward his ground-floor apartment.

As he reached the door, the overgrown shrubbery sneezed.

Alex froze.

All right, he was haggard. Totally wiped out. As tuckered as Rip Van Winkle. But he had realized since the inquisitive age of three that bushes did not sneeze.

Shaking his head, he returned his attention to the door lock. A breeze rustled the huge shrub.

A rustle, not a sneeze.

He *wasn't* going bonkers.

He slipped the key into the lock.

'*Hee-yah!*' The bush launched off the side of the house and landed on his back.

'Wha — ?' Alex stumbled against the doorjamb. His computer case fell to the stoop as the hundred-plus-pound weight clinging to his spine bounced left and squealed. Green legs gripped his hips, pinning his arms. An elbow cinched his throat. He glimpsed a silver gun twinkling in the pale light. An instant later, a black hood shrouded his head.

A second attacker whipped a rope around his wrists, pulled them behind his back, and rapidly bound them.

Heart pounding, Alex sucked in a breath. Fabric plastered his mouth. Slim fingers knotted the hood behind his neck. Some *kid* — some teenagers — had ambushed him?

'Get the hell off me!' He thrust back his shoulders, but the kid's legs squeezed tight. His assailant boasted the build of a gymnast — small, compact, and wiry-strong. Yet, in some places, curiously soft.

'I don't think so,' the boy whispered in an obviously lowered voice. He poked the gun into Alex's neck. Adolescent vocal chords cracked.

'Please. Cooperate with me, and you won't get hurt.'

'*Me?*' Alex struggled to slow the adrenaline pumping through his veins. *Think!* ''Me' generally means one. There are at least two of you.'

What sort of muggers pleaded for cooperation? Demanding money, Alex understood. But begging indicated desperation. And desperation was dangerous.

Were his attackers on drugs?

He'd give these loser punks whatever they wanted. He wouldn't risk his life over the measly thirty bucks in his wallet.

'Try my back pocket,' he told the kid.

'Why would I do that?' the kid asked.

'Nicky, lift your butt,' the second boy whispered.

Nicky grunted and shifted higher on Alex's back. Small, soft bumps pressed into Alex's spine.

Bumps?

His stressed mind whirred.

A stretching-and-ripping sound filled

13

the air. *Tape. Thick tape*. In Mugger Number Two's possession.

They planned to rope *and* tape him? What was next? A little recreational tarring and feathering?

At least Alex knew one boy's name now. *Nicky*. Maybe a sense of familiarity would help calm the dunce.

'Wait,' he said evenly. 'You don't have to tape me. I'll cooperate. Nicky . . . ' Alex didn't dare turn his head. Not with cold steel biting his neck and Mugger Number Two awaiting the green light to wrap and seal him like a Christmas package destined for a turbulent ride through the mail. 'That's your name, right? Nicky? What you want is in my pocket.'

Now would be a perfect time for his landlords to arrive home. Or for someone driving down the alley to spot him and rush to his aid.

However, the afternoon-shift workers he rented from never failed to park out front, and the fences and overgrown shrubbery shielded his apartment door.

He'd always appreciated the extra privacy — until today.

Nicky's shallow breathing panted in his ears. The kid moved, and the elbow cinching Alex's throat loosened.

'I don't want what's in your pocket, you pervert,' Nicky said hoarsely. 'I — *yikes! I'm falling!*'

The kid's voice broke on a high and distinctly female shriek. The mugger's squirming and the force of gravity toppled Alex and his assailant to the ground in a tangle of flailing limbs, soft bumps, and connecting concrete.

The gun bonked Alex's jaw, and a warped warbling slashed the air. Like a laser, or a phaser, or something equally space-movie-ish.

That hadn't been cold steel poking his neck! More like chilly plastic. These idiots had held him up with a toy gun. He groaned.

'Nicky!' Number Two wailed in undisguised female tones. A body part — knees? — thumped the ground. Alex sensed Number Two hovering over them. 'Are you okay?'

'Yeah,' Nicky — the female variety, which accounted for the soft bumps — murmured. 'I slipped.'

Alex's head rested on what felt like her stomach. The concrete chewed his bound hands, and the rope chafed his wrists. His knuckles hurt like a cheese grater had scraped off half their skin.

'Ooof.' Nicky wriggled beneath him. 'Could you please get off me?'

Her soft voice tweaked a memory. Beneath the hood, Alex squinted.

'Nicky?'

A visual of a petite woman blossomed: big blue eyes, porcelain skin, a sexy moptop of silvery-blond curls.

'*Nikki St. James?*' He rolled off her. Royce Carmichael's fiancée — the airheaded rich chick — had jumped him?

'Yes.' She sighed. 'How did you guess?'

Shoes scuffled on concrete. Her accomplice must be helping her up.

'Karin, you weren't supposed to say

16

my name,' Nikki admonished Number Two.

'Sorry,' the woman named Karin replied.

'Don't worry about it. We have him where we want him. That's the main thing.'

Alex rolled his eyes as his vision adjusted to the hood. Something wacky must be going on, because Nikki St. James was as wacky as they came, according to her fiancé. Royce had bragged about Nikki's affinity for fun and games when Alex had last met his old friend for drinks over the winter. Party games, mind games, sex games — apparently, Nikki enjoyed them all.

Royce had made a point of describing her proclivities to Alex and then had outlined the perks of their non-exclusive relationship, despite Alex's attempts to change the subject.

To Alex, the sexual freedom of the couple's arrangement sounded like trashy reality TV — one of those series where a group of strangers lived

17

together, went clubbing every night, and slept around.

He'd always had difficulty pairing Nikki's angelic looks and air of natural innocence with the blonder-than-a-blonde-joke image Royce promoted. However, at the moment, she wasn't doing much to dispel her reputation.

He gritted his teeth. 'What's this about?'

Two sets of female hands grabbed his arms and dragged him to standing.

'Ugh,' Nikki gasped, clutching his shoulder. 'You're heavy.'

No duh. He must have seventy pounds on her. '*You're* tiny.' She hadn't answered his question. 'What . . .' He injected steel into his voice '. . . is this about?'

'That's simple. I'm kidnapping you. Karin, please pass me the duct tape.'

Alex's mental light bulb snapped on. Okay, *now* he got it. The idea was so asinine, it made perfect sense. Barely-standing-five-foot-two and bubble-headed-eyes-of-blue was throwing Royce a bachelor party.

Forget that the couple had yet to announce a wedding date, Nikki St. James was ditzy enough to throw her fiancé a bachelor party instead of allowing the best man the honors — and then screw up the festivities by abducting Alex for the crazy night ahead instead of kidnapping the groom.

'Look, I've had a rough week,' he said. 'I need to take it easy tonight. Tell Royce I can't make it.'

'Um . . . '

'What's he talking about?' Karin whispered.

'Shh,' Nikki murmured. 'Alex, you have to come. You're the cheese.'

Cheese? 'You mean a trap to lure Royce to the party?'

'Ummm . . . '

His right eyelid twitched. 'You're telling me Royce doesn't know about tonight yet, either?'

'Uh, nope. But he will soon.' Nikki's voice rose on a plaintive note Alex recognized from years of helping his two younger sisters deal with bonehead boyfriends. 'Please, I need your help. Tonight is an important step for me and Royce. I've arranged everything just so.'

Something in her tone ensnared him. That same aura of innocence that contradicted her reputation as a partier.

His big-brother instincts took over. *What a sucker.*

'Since you put it that way, don't sweat it. Do what you want to. I'll play.'

Her breath whooshed out. 'Thank you.'

The duct tape ripped near his ears. Alex failed to see the purpose of allowing her to tape him when his hands were already tied. However, considering that a second ago he'd promised to cooperate, he remained motionless while she and Karin bound his chest and arms with numerous passes of the thick tape — rendering him as agile as an Egyptian mummy.

'Can you see through the pillowcase?' Nikki asked.

He swore. So that was what she'd plunged over his head — an everyday pillowcase, not a hood.

Joke on him.

He peered through the black fabric. A petite figure stood in front of him. He nodded. 'What's on your head?' he asked.

She flipped a sock-shaped . . . thing out of her eyes. Some kind of mugger's mask mashed her delicate features.

'Pantyhose?' His mouth quirked.

She ignored his question. 'You can see. Darn it. Now you'll guess where we're going.'

'I'll close my eyes.'

'I can't trust you yet. Sorry. You can close them for me now, though.'

Alex shut his eyes.

'Good. Please lower your head.'

He did. And felt her tie a blindfold over the pillowcase. Double darkness.

'Point me in the direction of the donkey,' he murmured, feeling as disoriented as a nine-year-old subjected to Pin-the-Tail torture.

'No donkey. Just my van.'

'You mean that ancient Econoline

parked in the alley? Isn't it turn-of-the-century?'

'Yes. Thanks for noticing! It's a '96.'

'No kidding.' Alex had wondered who owned the shabby white behemoth. Never in a million years would he have guessed Nikki. Not when daddy-dermatologist with the patented miracle wrinkle cream bought his little princess anything she desired.

Or so Royce had mentioned.

'Karin, his keys and laptop case,' Princess Nikki directed her friend. 'Slip the keys inside your — '

'Don't say it,' Karin whispered.

'Oh, right. Gotcha.'

Both women stepped several feet away. 'Yes, that's perfect.' Nikki's quiet voice carried on the afternoon breeze. 'That. And that.'

Alex cocked an ear. 'What and what?'

'Nothing for you to worry about,' she called.

He'd still like to know!

The women returned. 'We'll take your case with us,' Nikki said. 'I don't want someone happening along and thinking there'd been a struggle here or anything.'

He snorted. 'Even though there was?'

The women escorted him to the alley, Nikki gripping one arm and Karin the other. When they stopped, he did. Nikki released his arm, and the rear van doors clacked open. Something scuffled inside the van.

'Fellas, this is the guy I told you about,' Nikki said. 'Everyone stay quiet and make room. Bernie, that means you.'

The partier named Bernie whined as the women hoisted Alex into the van. Had Nikki gagged the guy? How many of Royce's friends had these nutty chicks grabbed for tonight's party, anyway?

Alex couldn't tell, but a second fellow — a hulk of a man squatting beside him — lacked good oral hygiene. The oaf needed to brush his teeth. Badly. Like with a thermos brush.

'Lie down,' Nikki ordered.

Assisted by Karin, Alex obeyed. He didn't have a choice, really. Nikki's melodic voice was impossible to resist.

His legs protruded out of the van. As he sensed her leaning over him, his skin buzzed. She untied his wrists and pulled off the rope.

'Thanks.' Only the tape binding his arms remained. 'Have you taped all of us?'

'No.' *Rrrriiiip.* 'Just you.' She pushed up the legs of his pants and mummy-wrapped his ankles.

'Come on, Nikki, you don't have to do that. I promised I'd cooperate.' He wriggled on the rough van carpeting.

'I'm not taking any chances.' She rubbed the duct tape, sealing it.

Bernie whined again — then barked. A high-pitched, yappy, toy-breed sound.

'Bernie,' Nikki scolded. 'Shh.'

'Bernie's a *dog?*'

She didn't refute the obvious. Her footsteps scuffed back, and she whispered something indecipherable to Karin.

A sharp meow carried from above Alex's head. His jaw hardened. 'Let me guess. That's a cat.'

'His name's Rusty.' Nikki leaned over him again. She bent his legs, then closed one of two back doors he'd noticed on the vehicle the other day. 'Don't worry, Rusty won't scratch you. He's in his cat carrier.'

'That's a relief.' What kind of *lunatic* took animals to a bachelor party?

Halitosis Hal loomed over the pillow-case, practicing his heavy breathing.

Plip.

Make that heavy drooling. *Agh!*

'You don't have a sheep in here, do you?'

'No,' Nikki answered. 'Why would I?'

'I don't know. Maybe Royce likes that sort of thing.' *Don't go there.* 'Never mind.' Alex inched away from hairy, hulking Hal — whoever, *whatever* Hal's mammalian orientation. 'Listen, Nikki, I need some reassurance here. I realize tonight is for Royce and all that, but I'm getting some weird

25

vibes. Couldn't you at least let me know *where* you're holding this bachelor party?'

For a moment, she didn't respond.

Then, 'Who said anything about a bachelor party?'

The second rear van door slammed shut.

2

The Get-Away

Hands shaking, Nikki jammed a key into the rear double-door lock. Her heart had commandeered permanent residence in her throat, the pounding in her ears so loud she feared her conscience would go deaf. That was, if it hadn't fainted dead away by now.

'What? No bachelor party?' Alex's muffled voice carried through the closed van doors. 'Why the hell did you tape me up?'

She locked him in. Practically wheezing from the strain of breathing through nylon, she peeled off the mask and gulped in fresh air. Her hair sprang free of the nylon, her follicles screaming abuse. Behind her, Karin cursed.

'Nikki!' Alex yelled. 'Answer me, or I'll kick through these doors!'

Loud thumps indicated that the supposedly mild-mannered history professor meant business. Bernie's yapping echoed inside the van she'd inherited from her grandfather, and Rusty yowled as if auditioning for an opera. Only Santos, dependable Santos, possessed the presence of instinct to remain mum.

Nikki banged the doors. 'Quiet in there! Please! Alex, just stay calm.'

'Calm? *Calm?* How do you expect me to stay calm when you have me trussed like a turkey for your latest trip down Loony Lane?'

Loony? Did he think she was unbalanced? 'Alex, I promise I won't hurt you. If you give me a minute to finish up, I'll explain my plan.'

But she wouldn't give him the option to un-volunteer. Despite this afternoon's evidence to the contrary, she hated deception and pretense. She'd done enough pretending in her life, enough waiting patiently, enough striving to please others to gain their love. Particularly with her own family.

She had to think about *her* needs for once. About how Alex could help her jumpstart her inattentive fiancé.

His feet thumped against the doors, and the old van rocked. *Crap*.

Nikki turned to Karin. Her cousin had de-masked, as well, and Karin's hair winged around her head in fly-away strands. She looked like a poster child for victims of pantyhose static.

How fruitcakey. No wonder Alex seemed kinda anxious.

'He's not as cooperative as I'd hoped. We'd better leave.' Nikki handed Karin her mask in exchange for the rope. 'Keep the gun. I don't need it anymore.'

Karin stared at the toy laser. 'What should I do with it?'

'Give it to a kid in your apartment building, save it for next Halloween, bash Royce over the head with it if he's too dense to figure out where Alex and I have gone.'

Karin shifted her feet. 'Yeah, Nikki,

what if Royce *doesn't* figure it out?'

'Then that's where you come in. If Royce can't read between the lines of my note — ' in which case, their relationship was in deeper hoo-hoo than she'd feared ' — it's up to you to point him in the right direction.'

'God, I don't know, Nik.'

'*I* do.' A lump swelled in her throat. She swallowed. 'If Royce is worried about me, he'll call or text. When he realizes I'm not answering, he'll contact you.' For the purposes of this weekend, she'd left her cheapo cell phone at home. Let Royce fight for their relationship for once. Knowing him, he'd appreciate the challenge. 'Karin, you and I are best friends. Royce might assume we talked about a hookup. The poor guy will need reassurance that I still want him. You know, if he . . . if he still wants me. If he wants me, he'll come get me.' She refused to consider what she would do if Royce didn't come after her. He would, and that was that.

Karin's lips pressed together. 'Should I log onto your web account and change your relationship status?'

'No! My sister would freak.' Pretty sad when social networking was her major link to Gillian. 'Worse, she'd grab the opportunity to blab my problems to our parents. I don't want to kill my relationship with Royce. I want to save it.'

Karin nodded. 'Understood.'

Nikki hugged her cousin. 'Thank you, Kare. I love you.'

'Love you, too.'

Behind them, Alex's thuds and muffled protests grew louder. The van rocked and squeaked like a bed getting broken in by honeymooners. Rusty wailed, and Bernie yowled.

Nikki sighed. 'I have to leave before he ruins my suspension. Do you have enough cab fare?'

'Yes. Good luck, Nik. I hope you get what you want out of all this.'

'So do I.' Nikki squeezed her cousin one last time, then strode to the driver's door and lifted the handle. Her heart beat an erratic rhythm.

Here goes something.

★   ★   ★

Blind as a bat but lacking the compensating radar, Alex struggled against the duct tape binding him. A front van door opened and closed. The engine sputtered before roaring to life, and the van careened down the alley.

The yappy mutt named Bernie yanked on Alex's pants leg while the cat howled a horrifying nails-scratching-brick-walls sound. Hairy Hal took the van's start as a sign to cease slobbering on the pillowcase.

'Nikki!' Alex's gut churned as the van screeched to a halt, swerved right, then peeled out of the alley. 'Hey! Slow down! There are kids in this neighborhood!'

'Sorry!'

His abductor reduced speed. *Responds well to orders, does she?*

Hadn't Royce once mentioned how much Nikki loved it when a man took charge?

Whatever works.

'Nikki, stop this van! You stop this van *right now*.' Alex adopted the same firm tone his father had used when disciplining him and his sisters on the farm.

'No can do.'

So much for what Royce had said. 'Why the hell not?'

'I already told you.'

Alex pressed the rewind button in his over-stressed mind. 'You're kidnapping me. For a bachelor party.'

Correction, Hart. No bachelor party.

A hollow sickness twisted in his chest.

'You're *kidnapping* me? Federal felony kidnapping?'

'No! Oh my God! Not seriously kidnapping. More like seriously borrowing. Alex, I need your help.'

He chopped out a laugh. 'You could have asked.'

'I *am* asking. This is me . . . this is me asking.' Her voice thickened with the threat of tears. As an experienced older brother, Alex recognized the signs.

'Karin, can't you talk some sense into her?' he petitioned her friend. 'You don't want to be an accomplice.'

'You're wasting your breath. Karin's not here.'

'She isn't?' Right, he hadn't heard the clicking of the passenger door opening and closing before they'd torn out of the alley.

'Nope. I sent her home. And I'll never admit she helped me.'

Great. A quick recap: he was hooded and duct-taped in the back of a speeding van with a party girl in mid-crisis at the wheel, a growling dog yanking his pants leg, Rusty the Yowling Wonder Cat, and Halitosis Hal breathing all over him.

As Friday afternoons went, Alex had rarely experienced worse. And it looked like Friday night was gearing up to be one frantic ride.

Forget beer and pizza. Yeah, he'd wanted downtime, but downtime he controlled, not this wacky blonde.

He had lists to write, research to do. The university's history library called his name. He really should heed that call.

But first he needed to stop this Nikki Express and jump off.

'Alex, please try to understand.' Her voice lifted above the cat's meows. 'I need to get Royce's attention. I need him to worry about me. And how I feel about him. So he'll come after me.'

'Come after *you*? I'm the one being kidnapped.' Grunting, Alex stretched down his bound arms while straining his bent legs up behind his thighs. His ribs ached from when he'd stumbled against the doorjamb. He skipped his fingers over the duct tape in search of a loose flap. His hand bonked Bernie's head. *Damn*.

The dog yelped, releasing his pants leg. Tiny paws scrambled up, over, and around Alex's feet. Frenzied yipping filled the van.

'Alex! I can see you in the rearview mirror!'

Damn it.

The van slowed. 'I untied your wrists for comfort,' Nikki warned. 'Don't make me regret doing so.'

'Or what? You'll set hairy Hal on me?'

'Who?' A pause elapsed. 'Oh. His name's not Hal, it's Sant — ' Bernie's yipping swallowed her soft voice.

'Santa?'

'Santos,' she corrected. 'Although, that's pretty quick thinking on your part, Alex. He did come to me at Christmas, and he does kind of remind me of a big, jolly Santa Claus. That's why I named him Santos.'

'Wonderful.'

'I'm glad you agree. Now, please be quiet and lie still. I need to watch the traffic.'

She really did have a screw loose. As did the hyperactive Bernie. The little dog raced up Alex's chest, then jumped off to tug the pillowcase. Alex angled his head, but the growling mutt tugged harder.

'Stop that, you mangy — ' The blindfold loosened on the pillowcase, and Alex stiffened. *Hmm.* Rolling onto his side, he wrenched his chin forward.

Bernie yanked, and Alex wrenched again. The blindfold slackened, slithering down the pillowcase. Again, Bernie tugged, and the pillowcase inched up Alex's face. His pulse raced.

He lifted his head off the carpet. Bernie growled and tugged.

That's it, Yapper. Come on, boy. Keep going.

The dog pulled and yanked until the pillowcase rode Alex's nose. Air blasted his nostrils. *Yes!*

Yipping, Bernie abandoned the pillowcase. Tiny feet scampered to approximately level with Alex's chin. Fabric *swooshed* on carpet, but the pillowcase — apparently no longer a challenge — stayed put.

Think you've bested me, mutt?

Alex scrunched his nose, jerked his chin, and thrust back his head.

Scrunch, jerk, thrust. Scrunch, jerk, thrust again.

The pillowcase now roosted on his eyebrows. *Good enough.*

Head scarcely moving, he surveyed the interior of the van. Black garbage bags coated the back windows, and the rear seats had been removed, increasing cargo space. Thick carpeting padded the old metal chair anchors. Lucky thing or painful gouges would decorate his back by now.

Near his feet, a Mexican Chihuahua — the yappy Bernie, no doubt — sat chewing a large red kerchief, a.k.a. the blindfold. The sort of thing kids playing cowboy wore around their necks.

To the side, a roomy pet carrier jailed a chocolate-faced, sapphire-eyed Siamese cat. *Rusty.*

Ribs aching, Alex shifted. A deep woof boomed behind him.

Channeling his inner ninja, he silently rolled over. Rheumy brown eyes gazed at him from the russet-masked face of a senior-citizen Saint Bernard.

'Santos?' he whispered.

The dog's huge head tipped. 'Woof?'

Unbelievable. Any normal person would have called the Saint Bernard 'Bernie' and retained the Spanish 'Santos' for the miniature jumping bean currently on a chewing break — but not Royce Carmichael's fiancée.

If Nikki had hatched tonight's scheme with the same lack of logic she employed naming animals, Alex was in serious trouble.

At least Santos possessed a calm nature, a certain old-dog dignity that balanced Bernie's canine ADD. And Nikki's wackiness.

Well, maybe not the latter.

Digging his heels into the carpeting, Alex arched his back and twisted his neck to gain sight of his captor. Her slim hands gripped the steering wheel, her engagement ring glittering in the pale afternoon light. Her profile show-cased the porcelain skin he yearned to touch each time he saw her. Today, despite the circumstances, proved no exception.

Sap. He hadn't had a date in so long it appeared he was in danger of developing the hots for his abductor. An engaged abductor, no less. His old buddy's fiancée.

In other words, hands off.

Royce and Nikki might not live by conventional morals, but he did.

The van slowed as they approached a red light — the perfect escape opportunity. If he didn't break free now, he could be stuck in this maniac menagerie for hours.

He couldn't rouse Nikki's suspicions, though. He had to play this right.

Breathing in and out through his nose, he lay quiet until the van came to a complete stop. Seattle was famous for congested traffic. In all likelihood, a thick snake of vehicles trailed behind them.

He kicked his bound feet against the van doors. Bucking up and down, he yelled, 'Help! Somebody help me! I'm being kidnapped!'

Nikki screeched. 'Alex, stop that! You're giving me a heart attack!'

Bernie seconded her motion. The dog raced back and forth across Alex's chest, barking. The cat squalled, and Santos's hefty paw batted Alex's shoulder. 'Woof?'

'Alex, I'm warning you!' Radio static blasted the van. A warped medley of DJ chatter and loud music streamed from the speakers until Nikki located a station. A woman's voice belted out the pain of betrayal, the power notes drowning Bernie's barks — and Alex's banging.

Nikki sang along, her voice too cheerful for his liking.

'I love this song! Best of all, no one can hear you now. To the cars around us, I'm just lost in my music. So you might as well relax.'

The van tore out of the intersection.

Chest heaving, Alex stopped kicking.

Damn it, she was right. Besides, he needed to gather his reserves before they reached another stop.

His face burned with exertion, and his hands throbbed from grinding into the carpet. At some point, the pillowcase had shaken off. Bernie sat nearby, chewing the stupid thing. Behind the tiny dog, groceries overflowed two cardboard boxes.

Alex blinked. How long did Nikki plan to keep him?

'Where are you taking me?' he bellowed.

'To my summer place. That's all I can say for now, so please don't ask again or try to trick me. I'm sorry, Alex. I realize this is inconvenient for you, but I didn't know what else to do.'

Her voice swelled with tears, and his chest tightened. He'd heard of Stockholm Syndrome, but this was ridiculous. No man in his right mind would sympathize with his abductor this early in the kidnapping game — if

42

at all. The rat race of the spring semester must have addled his brain.

He latched onto the meager information she'd released. They were heading to her summer place. Translation: a rich chick's haven.

Royce should know the location. He'd likely visited the place a dozen times.

And hadn't she said the purpose of her plan was to get Royce to chase after her? Or something equally cockeyed.

Alex had to remain optimistic.

Turning on his side, he glimpsed her reflection in the rearview mirror. With her blue eyes fever-bright and her blonde curls bobbing, she looked like a cross between the vintage kewpie dolls his mother collected and a toy poodle on amphetamines. He couldn't afford to upset her further, or she might go completely wiggy, careen off the road, and kill them all.

'Royce keeps postponing setting the wedding date,' she said, voice squeaking. 'We're seeing less of each other lately, and I'm getting worried.'

Alex shook his head. Naturally, Royce was avoiding the actual *marriage*. The engagement was a sham, a façade of respectability behind which Alex's old friend could conquer his career goals while Nikki partied hearty.

Didn't she realize that?

He frowned.

She continued, 'I left a note at my place saying you and I might hook up. We have a date tonight — Royce and me, not you and me. When he arrives, I won't be there.'

'You said we're *hooking up?*' She was insane!

As if in her defense, Santos woofed and nudged Alex's shirtsleeve. Wet dog nose chilled his shoulder.

'I haven't told him *yet*,' Nikki said beneath the radio. 'The note . . . ' She cleared her throat. 'The note will tell him.'

She'd left a freaking *note?*

Alex couldn't believe this — didn't want to. Either Nikki St. James had totally lost it or she wasn't anywhere near the sex-obsessed party girl Royce had described.

'I take it this note also mentions where we're going,' he muttered.

'Not really. But Royce will figure it out. The note says we're planning on exploring our attraction at my special place. Royce understands that's my gran — uh, my summer house. If by chance he doesn't put it all together, I'll know he . . . doesn't love me anymore.' She choked out a sob.

Alex's chest pinched. Had Royce led her on? He didn't want to believe his former college roommate capable of such blatant manipulation, but Royce's history with women worked against him. Unless, in typical ditz fashion, Nikki had crossed her wires — and now Alex suffered for it.

For the sake of wrongly maligned males everywhere, he latched onto the latter.

'But Royce *does* love me,' Nikki said. 'He has to. When he reads the note, he'll immediately realize where we've gone. He'll understand how badly he's neglected our relationship and how much he needs me. Then he'll come rescue me from your evil clutches.' She flicked a glance in the rearview. Her dimples flashed. 'Anyway, that's the plan.' Flipping on the blinkers, she announced, '1-5, here I come.'

'The freeway? We're not heading out of town, are we? Nikki, that's kidnapping beyond city limits!'

The radio blared louder. 'Sorry, I can't hear you!'

'Damn it.' Alex strained against the duct tape. Bernie, dragging the pillowcase, trotted over. The tiny mutt growled, and the pillowcase fell, covering Alex's face again. Santos barked and plopped two huge paws onto his stomach. The dog's boulder-sized head collapsed onto Alex's chest, pinning him.

His lungs squeezed beneath the Saint Bernard's significant bulk. However, Santos, evidently as immovable as the

Rock of Gibraltar, snuggled his hairy head into the crook of Alex's neck. The beast panted.

Dead-cat-for-lunch breath drifted.

Alex moaned. He couldn't move. He couldn't see. His ribs ached, and he could barely breathe.

And Nikki thought Royce should rescue her?

Alex knew better.

He was the one who needed rescuing.

★   ★   ★

Four harrowing hours later, Nikki pulled up to the rustic summer cabin she'd inherited from her grandparents along with the van. The drive to Washington's Olympic Peninsula ordinarily took half as long. However, needing to disorient Alex, she'd bypassed the ferries in favor of trekking down the freeway and then up Highway 101.

The tactic had better work. Between

the man's complaining and his unan-
ticipated knack for bringing out the
worst in her animals, her nerves rode a
frazzled edge.

Relaxing in her seat as the van idled,
she drank in the view. The last
tangerine smears of sunset traced the
sky above the forested hills and
reflected off the glassy surface of Lake
Eden. The old dock she'd learned to
dive from needed a few boards
replaced, but remained intact.

During her and Gillian's summer
visits with Gram and Gramps Sorensen,
Nikki had grown to love this place. Now,
the peaceful seclusion of the mountain
lake drew her into its night-gathering
embrace. With its narrow, dirt road approach
and the blackberry vines overgrowing
the back wall, the cabin provided an
ideal choice for an intimate, romantic
honeymoon.

At least she thought so. Royce wasn't
convinced. *Yet*.

Once her fiancé rescued her from
making a fictional mistake with Alex,

he'd change his mind about the cabin. He'd understand why she'd rather honeymoon here than the expensive all-inclusive resort he'd suggested. And he'd realize they both needed more out of marriage than a replication of her parents' passionless union: her father doling out scraps of affection when it suited his professional reputation and her mother never demanding more than the veneer of maintaining appearances.

'Are we there yet? Nikki, I'm dying back here!'

Alex's deep voice shattered her moment of peace. She switched off the engine and the headlights faded. The old van rumbled to sleep.

'Yes, we are.'

'It's about time. Let me out. And get this hairy mountain off my chest.'

'One second.' She retrieved the tangled rope from the passenger seat. 'Honestly, Alex, were you this much trouble for your mother as a child?'

A snort bulleted from the back of the van. 'My mother wasn't in the habit of disguising me as King Tut and carting me around the countryside. Farm folks tend to stick a bit closer to home.'

Nikki swiveled in her seat. Although garbage bags covered the rear windows, the last shreds of twilight coming through the windshield faintly illuminated Alex. The pillowcase pooled beside his head, and his rumpled brown hair lent him an attractive, non-professorial appeal.

Santos slumbered on the poor guy's chest, further tarnishing her impression of Alex the Intellectual. In the corner, Rusty peered through his cat carrier. Near the carrier, Bernie panted on his side, the red blindfold draped over one tiny front paw like a pupster security blanket.

'A farm?' she asked. 'Sounds heavenly. My grandfather on my mother's side farmed near Poulsbo.' She named a community on the Kitsap Peninsula, west of Seattle, steeped in Norwegian-immigrant history. Aside from Gram and Gramps's fishing trips to Lake

Eden, the couple had rarely left the Poulsbo area until after Gramps retired.

Nikki's mother, on the other hand, had fled the farm for Seattle and Geoffrey St. James at eighteen. Despite Nikki's pleas, her mother had declared a strict no-pets zone in the St. James household.

'I love animals,' she murmured. 'I can't imagine a better childhood than growing up on a farm.'

'Yeah? Well, *I* can't imagine a worse demise than expiring in this portable zoo from inhaling noxious fumes. Are you going to dig me out from beneath Santa of the Smelly Breath or not?'

The guy was grumpy. Considering his situation, she couldn't blame him. She'd refused to leave any of her pets behind, though. Her two roommates had flown to Europe this morning, leaving their small rental house empty, and the veterinary office where she worked didn't have much boarding space. She hadn't felt right caging her perfectly healthy fellas in pens intended for animals recovering from surgery, especially after her boss had already given her a week off.

'Oh, come on. Santos's breath isn't toxic swamp gas. I haven't had a chance to brush his teeth in a couple of days, that's all. He's too old to put under anesthetic just for plaque removal.'

Alex's eyebrows snapped together. '*What?*'

'Okay, okay.' She opened her door. The interior light flashed on. 'I wasn't planning to leave you in here all night. We'll wait for Royce in the cabin.'

'Gee, thanks.'

She inhaled. 'Alex, tonight could be a pleasant experience for you. Really, it's your choice. Royce should arrive at my place any moment, which means he'll find the note soon. If he leaves Seattle right away, he'll get here in a matter of hours. If he waits until dawn to drive, he'll reach us in the morning, tomorrow afternoon at the latest. Now, we — you and me — can either pass the time genially or waste it bickering. I don't know about you, but I'd rather try to be friends. That means no more escape attempts and *no* snide remarks about Santos.'

The not-so-mild-mannered college professor grated out a humorless laugh. 'You actually believe you can keep me here against my will?'

'If that's how you want to be, I'll make sure of it.'

Grabbing a fresh roll of duct tape, she climbed out of the van. She slipped the roll over one wrist, then rewrapped the tangled rope and slung it onto her shoulder like a female Indiana Jones.

Breathing in the fresh lake air, she strode toward the rear van doors. Her foot hit an exposed tree root, and she paused.

What are you doing, Nikki?

Ugh, just what she needed — her conscience chiming in.

Clearly, Alex was unhappy with her plan. Amend that, he was downright hostile.

Before tonight, she hadn't heard him

utter a single sarcastic word. And, at his apartment, once he'd assumed she'd nabbed him for a bachelor party, he'd cooperated like the good sport Royce recalled.

An upstanding guy like Alex Hart deserved more than to have his Friday night plans derailed. Even if, as Royce often mentioned, Alex was so preoccupied with pursuing tenure that he possessed the social life of a slug. Maybe after she prepared him a nice dinner, he'd lighten up.

Regardless of his attitude, she'd forge ahead. Her future with Royce depended on it.

She trod on.

Standing safely back from the van, she turned the key and opened a door a crack. 'Remember, Alex, I can lead a horse to water and I *can* make him drink. So don't test me. You'll have a decent time tonight if it kills me.'

'There's a thought,' he muttered from behind Santos's sweet head.

Ha, ha. 'In case you're dreaming of

54

tunneling out of here, you might want to keep in mind that you don't know where we are. And I won't tell you. In a few minutes, it will be black outside, and I believe there are coyotes lurking about.' She hadn't spotted a coyote at Lake Eden in her life, but the tale sounded good enough to continue spinning. 'Warthogs, rattlesnakes, poisonous centipedes — treacherous creatures abound. And don't get me started on the Stinging Prickleberries or the Queen Newt's Wort,' she fabricated. 'That stuff will turn your whole leg black if you step on it.'

'Then it's a good thing I'm wearing shoes.'

'Not anymore you're not.' She swung both doors wide, yanked off his loafers, and tossed them into the front.

The professor's crude response roused Bernie. The little dog's head popped up, and he blinked. One pupster yawn, an adorable stretch, and a departing growl in Alex's direction later, Bernie leapt out of the van and raced around Nikki's heels, barking.

'Bernie, take a tinkle.' She waved a hand. 'Find a bush, boy. Hurry, hurry.'

Compliant as always, the dog raced off and relieved himself.

Rusty — blue eyes narrow slits in the cat carrier — meowed.

Nikki gripped Alex's bound ankles. She straightened his legs and jostled them to alert Santos. 'Wake up, Santos. Out of the van now, fella. You can do it, big boy. Time to get up.'

Alex mumbled, 'I think his muscles have atrophied. Mine have.'

'Nonsense. Santos might be old, but he's not decrepit. And you're a . . . healthy specimen.'

'You don't say.'

Nikki studied his large frame. Yes, she most assuredly *did* say. At about six-foot-one, Alex towered over Royce when the two men stood together. However, what Royce lacked in height, he made up for with his boyish charm and dark good looks.

In contrast, Alex's features veered

toward the rugged. Not to-the-extreme, tobacco-spitting, tough-as-a-rangy-cowboy rugged, but rugged enough to suggest the tiller-of-the-earth background he'd mentioned.

Paired with his casually sexy professor vibe, Alex Hart was an intriguing man.

Intriguing, but not to her taste. Nope. Her heart belonged to one guy — Royce. Therefore, her libido also belonged to Royce.

Not that he'd taken much advantage of her libido lately. *Like going on over two months!*

But that was okay. She didn't need sex. She wanted love.

Her palms tingled from where they rested on Alex's khakis. Her fingers itched with the urge to move upward. Her face burned. Why did she have her hands all over this man's legs again?

Oh yeah, Santos.

She jostled Alex, and Santos's head lifted. Yawning, the big dog plodded out of the van. Sniffing the ground, the

Saint Bernard lumbered toward Bernie's bush.

Nikki tugged Alex's legs — and dragged him less than three inches. Grunting, she tried again. Epic fail!

She huffed out a breath. 'Alex, you could help.'

'How? That beast crushed my chest.'

'Take it as a compliment. Santos must like you.' She didn't seriously believe the old dog had hurt him. Not with Alex's leanly muscled hot bod evident beneath his amber dress shirt open at the collar.

The man just wanted to annoy her.

And he was doing a good job.

'Move it,' she ordered. 'We need to get you inside.'

Grabbing one of his pinned arms, she hauled him out of the van. He wobbled on the soft earth, knees buckling before he regained his balance.

'My legs are stiff.'

'Yeah, yeah.' But her face prickled. All of his extremities were probably . . . quite uncomfortable.

If only Royce's indecisiveness hadn't pushed her to this madness.

Gentling her grip, she helped Alex the few yards toward the cabin — amid much grumbling on his part as he shuffled sock-clad feet to the door.

She unlocked the cabin, and Bernie ran over from the bush. The Chihuahua darted into the dark interior, Santos following. The big dog's tail whapped her legs.

Nikki prodded her guest forward. 'I was here two weeks ago, checking the generator and cleaning up. We won't have to worry about the rattlesnakes or centipedes as long as we stay inside.'

Alex slanted her a glance. 'Been planning this caper awhile?'

'Not really.' She hadn't prepped the cabin with the borrowing in mind, but, rather, for a romantic weekend get-away with Royce. Her fiancé hadn't warmed to the idea, though; another indication they were growing apart.

It was then she'd realized she needed to do something drastic or risk losing

Royce altogether.

'Call it necessity born of inspiration,' she said as she flicked on the lights. 'I cleaned the cabin and *then* developed my strategy.'

'Hmph. Does this strategy include untaping me before Royce arrives?'

'Of course. I can't expect him to believe you came voluntarily otherwise.' Nikki peered at her guest. Was a sneaky glint lighting his hazel eyes? 'Don't get your hopes up, professor. I'm not leaving you any opportunities to escape. Yes, I'll untape you . . . ' Slipping the rope off her shoulder, she grinned. ' . . . right after I tie you up.'

3

The Captive Grows Restless

Alex shuffled deeper into the cabin as his captor closed the door behind them. She held the coiled rope calmly, her cupid-bow lips smiling. Her blue eyes sparkled with mischief and something resembling pride.

She actually thought she made sense! Somewhere in her beautiful blonde head of curls, her crazy kidnapping scheme possessed a loopy brand of logic.

'Oh no, you don't,' he stated. 'Not the rope again. No. Nikki, I've spent the last several hours taped like a human hockey stick. If you think I'll trade one form of torture for another, you're nuts.'

The corners of her mouth curved up. 'Sticks and stones, Alex,' she murmured in her soft, lyrical voice. 'I'm not a lunatic. I'm in love. You don't have to be afraid of me. I won't hurt you, but . . . I need you here. I have supplies to unload. Plus Rusty. I can't risk you running off while I'm back and forth to the van and stuff. I might be a while.' She placed the rope on a scarred wooden dining table, then dragged a mismatched chair to the center of the great room. The chair legs scraped the plank floor, painted a chipped and faded sky blue.

Bernie scampered alongside her, yipping at the rasping chair legs. His ears fanned back from his head like two miniature kites. His luminous brown eyes bulged.

Nikki planted the chair on the floor. 'I can't keep my eye on you every second while we wait for Royce to arrive,' she continued in a reasonable tone. 'I have to feed the animals and make dinner. So, I'm afraid your only choices are to stay taped or — ' she tapped the chair back ' — agree that you're fit to be tied.'

Alex's jaw tensed. Getting angry with her wouldn't solve anything. But being straightforward might help.

'I'm not afraid of you, okay? I'm fed up.' His fingers, hanging over his ass, stiffened. His arms ached with the need to gesticulate — a side effect from lecturing History 101 to often-disinterested freshmen — but the duct tape restrained his limbs as securely as a hospital patient in traction. 'I'm a busy man, with a busy life. Did you consider that when you grabbed me?'

Her gazed skipped away. 'Of course I considered it. I do have a conscience. That's why I planned our little trip for today.'

Her reasoning eluded him. He closed his eyes briefly, but no rays of insight dawned.

'You've lost me. Nikki, I'm tired. Not to mention starving. My nose is itchy, my shirt smells like dog slobber, and Bernie's incessant yapping has drilled a permanent hole in my brain. Please tell me something that makes sense.'

She blinked. 'You're saying I don't make sense?'

'I'm saying I don't *understand* what you're saying!'

She shook her head. 'Which part don't you get?'

'All of it. But feel free to start with the kidnapping.'

She shrugged, but she couldn't be dissuaded from her plan.

She was a woman on a mission. An airhead with an attitude. A beautiful, bubble-headed bundle of bafflement.

And he was at her mercy.

'All right.' She gazed at him. 'I chose today to grab you, because I *know* you're busy. You're a busy man, like you said. Busy, busy, busy. Too busy to take a break. Like Royce.' She strolled to the table and plunked down the tape. Picked up the rope. Unwrapped it. 'You inputted your grades today, right? And you're not teaching the first summer session. I know, because I checked. So, you see, I did consider your schedule before deciding which day you might wish to free up. I even watched your apartment for several afternoons to determine when you'd get home.' Another shrug. 'Not that it would have made much difference if I hadn't gone to all that trouble.'

Alex's head spun. Not from fatigue or from lack of food. But from over-exposure to Nikki. 'What?'

She strolled to the kitchen and rummaged through a light yellow drawer. When she returned with a pair of rusty scissors, Santos tagged along.

'It's as plain as the egg on your face, Alex.' She snapped the scissors. 'It's Friday night — the beginning of the weekend. You've heard of weekends? They're lovely. Most people think of them as opportunities to relax.' Her lips pursed. 'But not you. If you're anything like Royce — and you must be, or two old pals like you and he would see each other more often — you have a to-do list longer than the string of degrees following your name. Like Royce, you need your breaks arranged for you. And, I need your help. So I decided that tonight you should get a break.' Her dimples flashed. 'Consider it a gift. No thanks necessary.'

Alex's nostrils flared. It didn't take a genius to realize that Nikki had projected her resentment of Royce's heavy schedule onto him. And maybe onto all men who labored for a living, intellectually or otherwise.

He'd concede that he worked harder than he suspected was healthy. However, long ago he'd accepted that he needed to sacrifice a personal life in order to achieve tenure as quickly as possible. His entire family had scrimped and sacrificed so he could become the first American-born Hart to earn a college education, let alone a Ph.D. He owed it to his parents and sisters to make the most of his credentials. That meant sticking to the tenure track, even though the power politics drove him nuts.

'I'm in charge of my own breaks,' he

advised his scissors-wielding kidnapper. 'For your information, I wasn't planning to work this weekend. I wasn't planning to do anything but eat, sleep, and slack off.'

Her eyes brightened. 'If you weren't planning to work, what's the problem?'

'Isn't it obvious? Nikki, you made a choice on my behalf that you had no right to make.' Santos nosed Alex's thigh. As Saint Bernard drool dribbled down his khakis, the fabric clung to his skin like warm paste. He inched away from the old dog's fetid breath. 'My life isn't your business, just like yours isn't mine. If you and Royce are having problems, I'm sorry, but it's not my concern.'

She turned up a hand. 'But you're Royce's best man and his closest friend. Don't you care whether or not he's happy?'

How to answer that? The Royce Alex knew reveled in the freedom of his relationship with Nikki and how their engagement could pave his quick access to Easy Street. Nikki's father's dermatology clinic, where Royce practiced and yearned to make partner, garnered rave online reviews from every pimple-popping rich kid in Seattle. And those teens' wealthy mothers swarmed the city's luxury stores to purchase the Eternal You wrinkle cream for which Nikki's father held the patent.

As far as Alex could determine, Royce's primary purpose behind proposing to Nikki had *never* included marriage. Supposedly, she was cool with that.

However, tonight she didn't seem at all on-board with the situation. More and more, she came across like a woman Royce had bamboozled with his slick charm.

Poor girl.

Alex had always been a sucker for a damsel in denial. Paint the damsel with an angel innocence and his white-knight instincts took over every time. His sisters had trained him well in that regard.

But he couldn't allow himself to get sucked into the confusing vortex of Nikki's problems. She'd whisked him away from Seattle for her own purposes. Slammed the stress back into his stress-free Friday night with not one thought about how it might affect him beyond locating a convenient break in his schedule. Oh, and he couldn't forget, repackaging that break as a 'gift' to appease her conscience.

He wanted that stress gone. *Now.*

'Yes, I care if Royce is happy,' he lied. At this point, he didn't give a damn. 'But what difference does it make if he arrives to find me taped or tied? Either way, he'll realize that you restrained me by force, which is bound to alert him to the fact that I *didn't* come voluntarily. Nikki, the jig will be up as soon as he walks through the door. Your only solution is to untape me without tying me back up. Trust me when I say I won't take off.'

'Uh, sorry, no. I'd love to trust you, Alex, but . . . you didn't prove yourself trustworthy when we stopped at the red light, remember. All that bouncing around and shouting ... If Santos hadn't fallen asleep on your chest, you probably *would* have run off by now. I can't take the risk of not restraining you.'

'Nikki.'

'Sorry, I said no. Besides, the rope idea has merit. Rope is quicker to remove than tape. You know, for when we hear Royce's car. And rope might not seem as strange to Royce. If he barges in before I untie you, he, um, might think I tied you up on purpose, if you know what I mean.' A bright pink splashed her face.

'Spare me.' Unfortunately, he saw her point. For all he knew, Nikki and Royce bound each other on a routine basis.

A little bondage with your brie, baby? Yeah, he could buy it. A nutcase had abducted him. Tossing a dash of kink into the mix didn't seem out of the question.

'Chop-chop. Time's a-wasting.' She

snapped the big scissors open and closed. 'Is it Mr. Hart in the cabin with the duct tape or the rope?'

'The rope,' Alex grumbled without sounding *too* much like he wanted to commit murder.

'That's the spirit.' She gestured to the chair. 'Please sit, and we'll get on with this. Rusty will go bongo if I leave him in the van much longer.'

Alex shuffled to the chair. Oh yeah, he had her now. She thought she was so clever? She'd quickly discover otherwise. He'd play along, let her tie him up, then take advantage of the crappy knot-tying skills she'd displayed with the pillowcase and blindfold, and free himself as soon as she left to fetch her cat.

As he neared the chair, he scoped out the cabin. He'd expected Nikki's 'summer place' to showcase the ultimate in rich-chick luxury. Instead, the simple frame structure could work to his benefit. Screened windows ran the length of the wall facing the lake.

Bearing in mind that the entire place appeared to have been constructed circa mid-twentieth-century, he doubted any of the windows sported complicated locks. A windowless wall backed two double beds positioned behind the chair Nikki stood beside. A bedraggled moose head loomed over one bed, and a lamp perched on the shared night-stand.

To the left of the second bed, the great room extended behind the par-tially closed-off kitchen. An old upright piano — a weird choice of furniture for a summer cabin, but what the hell — hugged a wall.

He glimpsed another window around the corner, and the place might also feature a back door. Both presented possible avenues for escape.

He'd determine his next move after he'd done his Houdini. Hot-wiring the van or running into the forested hills where the battered Ford couldn't climb provided two viable options.

Although . . . he reached the chair

. . . racing into the hills might work best. Even without his shoes, he could outpace Nikki. Hopefully, once she discovered he'd escaped, she'd assume he'd headed for the unlocked van.

He could lock the doors from inside the vehicle, but she had the keys. They'd play I'll-lock-and-you-unlock until dawn before he accomplished the hot-wiring.

Forget that. The hills it was.

Pasting on a resigned grimace, he sat on the chair. His ribs throbbed from when she'd jumped him at the house, but not as bad as earlier. Likely, he'd just bruised them.

'Okay, I'm sitting,' he said. 'What happens now?'

'I'll tie you to the chair without untaping you first.' Circling him, she snapped the scissors. Santos sniffed a nearby couch, his big tail chopping the air. Bernie sat beside the chair and yawned.

Nikki's eyes narrowed. 'Hmm. I shouldn't need more duct tape, unless the rope doesn't hold. But it *should* hold. I don't see why it — '

'It'll hold fine. Let's do this.'

'Oh?' Her eyebrows lifted. 'Suddenly anxious, are you?'

'Suddenly ravenous. You promised dinner. I want it.'

'Patience, Dr. Hart. We'll get there.'

Stooping, she set down the scissors, then threaded the rope between his armpit and the duct tape. Her small breasts, covered with the dark green turtleneck, bumped his shoulder. Once, twice.

Her fingers grazed his skin through the fabric of his shirt. Soft curls brushed his head, and the green-apple scent of her shampoo drifted to him.

Or was that her summery perfume?

Or the pure essence of Nikki?

His stomach clenched.

Hunger pangs.

She looped the rope around the chair and below his other armpit, then stood and stepped back, nibbling her thumbnail. After picking up the scissors, she cut the tape binding his arms and torso a couple of inches on either side, peeled it down, and wrapped another width of white rope around his chest.

Snip, peel went the duct tape. *Swoosh*, loop went the rope.

Bits of shirt lint clung to the stripped tape hanging off his chest. The gluey tang of adhesive pierced his nostrils. He smelled like a scratch-and-sniff magazine ad for 3M, and his skin itched like he'd dived into a patch of poison ivy.

As she cut the tape, it landed in sticky gray bunches on the floor. Holding his breath, he puffed out his chest and flexed his pecs so the rope would wrap looser than she intended.

Several crafty chest-puffs on his part later, she finished peeling and looping. She grasped his hands and positioned his arms to hang over the chair back.

Then she made a classic rookie mistake — and bound his wrists behind the chair within finger-touching distance of the chunky knot.

As she fumbled with the knot, Alex

suppressed a grin. This was so easy, he almost felt sorry for her. He'd destroy her handiwork as soon as she stepped out the door. She'd mentioned she might take a while — due to 'stuff.' He had no clue what 'stuff' entailed, and he didn't care as long as 'stuff' allowed him time to escape.

'Now your feet,' she said, kneeling before him. 'I need to untape your ankles before I can tie them to the chair legs.' She looked up. Tiny, light green earrings too pale for emeralds sparkled from her dainty earlobes. 'Earlier, you said I could trust you. I need you to prove that to me now, Alex. You won't kick me while I'm untaping your feet, will you?'

He snorted. 'What kind of guy do you take me for?' Despite her crazy kidnapping scheme, he couldn't physically hurt her. She'd be hurt soon enough when she discovered him gone and she needed to make up another story for Royce.

She smiled. 'Just checking.'

Shoving up his pants legs, she inserted the scissors between his taped ankles. *Snnnnniiiiiip.* The scissors blades flashed.

She placed the scissors on the floor, grabbed both ends of the split duct tape — and yanked.

'Ow!' Alex's ankles burned.

'Sorry! I tried to wrap the tape over your socks, but it caught your skin.' She hoisted the tattered strips of duct tape. Dozens of leg hairs stuck to the strips.

'Damn it, Nikki, couldn't you have been a little gentler? I didn't sign up for a chest wax.'

'Leg wax,' she corrected. 'Men can be such babies. It's no worse than ripping off a bandage. And it's over now, so why dwell on it?'

Crouching with her pert ass kissing the air, she retrieved the rope dangling from his wrists and passed the remaining corded length under the chair. One limb at a time, she looped his shins to the chair legs, then tied a second lumpy knot between his feet.

Standing, she dusted off her hands. 'Time to get Rusty.' She picked up the scissors and transferred them to the table. 'Santos, Bernie . . . boys, watch Alex.'

Bernie, upon hearing his name, lifted his head and whined. Santos tramped over from the couch and panted.

Nikki looked at Alex. 'Now, you . . . ' She wagged a finger. 'Don't *you* go anywhere.'

'Where would I go?' Alex asked, widening his eyes.

When she turned away, he grinned.

★　★　★

Rusty's miffed meow issued from the cat carrier as Nikki lugged the unit to the cabin stoop. A light drizzle had begun falling while she'd hidden the van's distributor cap beneath a loose board at the front of the building, and the air swelled with the fresh scent of springtime. If Alex happened to run off while she needed to visit the outhouse or accompany the dogs on an evening romp, he'd discover he couldn't start her self-vandalized van.

And people thought her airheaded. She'd planned this weekend to a tee.

Example, before fetching Rusty, she'd carted Alex's computer case to the door, along with the boxes of supplies she'd packed for her short vacation with Royce. However, the case no longer contained Alex's laptop or cell phone. Back in Seattle, while he'd stood waiting with the pillowcase covering his head, she'd relinquished both devices to Karin's care.

As added insurance, she had no plans to supply him with the glasses Karin had noticed tucked into the computer case. According to Royce, Alex only wore them for driving, so she wasn't condemning him to a severely myopic existence.

'*Mrrowwr.*' Rusty nosed the carrier door.

'Poor fella,' Nikki soothed. 'You've been cooped for hours. Not to worry,

Rusty-mine, I'll set up your litter box first thing.'

Stepping around the supplies on the stoop, she opened the cabin door. 'Oh!' Her dogs had mauled Alex in her absence!

Tied to the chair, Alex lay flat on his back, the chair legs propping his limbs. Santos licked the man's forehead, while Bernie growled and tugged his socks. Alex swore, and the dog stopped tugging.

Yipping, Bernie scampered beside the chair, lifted his leg . . . and watered Alex's khakis.

Nikki gasped. 'Bernie, stop that!'

She plunked the pet carrier on the table. Racing to Alex, she shooed away Bernie. With a yelp, the Chihuahua danced off, jumped onto the bed nearest the windows, and barked at Murray the moose head.

Santos continued licking Alex's forehead.

'Alex, I'm sorry!' Nikki skidded onto her knees beside the chair. 'Omigod, what happened?'

His eyes bulged. 'Your dog *peed* on me!'

'I know, I know! I can see that!'

Bernie's piddle stained the thigh of Alex's pants a dark soldier green. An inch away, a tiny puddle polished the floor.

Thankfully, in her hurry to reach her guest, she hadn't closed the door. Rain-scented air streamed into the cabin, counterbalancing the acrid aroma of Bernie's tinkle.

'Alex, I'm sorry. I'm embarrassed, and I'm really sorry. He didn't mean it.'

'Oh, he meant it. He just did it.'

'You don't understand.' She urged Santos away from the poor man's head. She ran into the kitchen, grabbed a rag and dampened a tea towel, then returned to kneel beside him. She wiped his forehead with the tea towel and sopped Bernie's puddle with the rag. 'Bernie went outside before we came in. He never has to go again so soon afterward. This . . . ' She plucked

the soaked fabric off Alex's leg. *Ick*.
' . . . was an act of pure aggression.'

The professor grunted. 'That's what I said.'

'No, you don't get it. Bernie's protective of me.' She revisited the kitchen to rinse the rag, continuing to explain, 'His first owner abused him terribly. When I adopted him, he was terrified — of me, of everyone he met. I'm the first human he's grown to like. It took ages before he trusted my roommates, and he's never warmed up to Royce. He's pretty much a one-woman dog.' Back in the main room, she dabbed Alex's pants with the wet rag. 'He misbehaves if he thinks someone is a threat to me or if they're acting irrational.'

'Why doesn't he go psycho around you then?'

She arched her eyebrows. 'Because, *he* doesn't think *I'm* irrational. Apparently, though, he thinks you are. He hasn't acted out like this in two years. You must have provoked him.'

She pressed the rag to Alex's pants and wiped. Hard thigh muscles bunched beneath the khakis, and tingles spread through her hands. A most unsettling sensation.

Holding her breath, she glanced at the least-muscled portion of Alex's body — his sock-clad feet.

Her gaze fell onto his lower pants leg. A four-inch tear marred the khakis.

She peered at him. 'What happened here, anyway?' She dropped the rag.

'What it looks like — your dogs attacked me. I was sitting quietly, minding my own business, when Peewee decided my pants *and* my socks would make a tasty treat. My pants ripped in the battle. Then Santos jumped up to breathe in my face, the chair tipped, and I fell. The rest, as we history professors like to say, is history.'

'Your hands!' She lowered her head to examine the damage.

'Forget my hands. It's my skull that's throbbing.'

'I brought ibuprofen.' She peeked into the space between the chair spindles and the floor. A tampered knot and slack rope greeted her.

Rocking back on her heels, she gaped at Alex. 'You untied the rope! You said I could trust you! I can't leave you alone for two minutes — '

'It was fifteen.'

' — and you try to escape. My dogs didn't attack you. They were *guarding* you.'

Why wouldn't he cooperate? Her plan was so simple.

She wiped a hand across her forehead. 'Alex, you know how important tonight is to me. I've tried my best to explain it.'

'Well, excuse me for not falling in line. This escapade wasn't my idea.'

He kept throwing the borrowing in her face. He had every right to, but that didn't mean she had to like it.

'I'm sorry about your pants. I'll buy you two pairs to replace them, if you'll cooperate.'

Rusty meowed from inside the carrier while Bernie barked at the moose head. Santos wandered outside.

Retrieving the rag, Nikki scrubbed the stained khakis. It was useless. Bernie's marking-mix was made of sturdy stuff.

'This isn't going to work.' She tossed down the rag again. 'These pants need soaking. You'll need to take them off.'

Alex's neck tendons tightened. 'They'll be opening a ski hill in *hell* before I remove my pants with that appendage-grabbing mutt hanging around. Who knows what he'll decide to latch onto next.'

An image of Alex's . . . privates sprang to mind. How would he compare to Royce in that department? Of course, she barely remembered what Royce's 'appendage' looked like, so rarely had she seen it.

Her face heated. She stared down her nose at her guest. 'My dog is not a pervert.'

'He's a borderline psychopath. That's enough.'

'Fine. You have three choices. One, you can wear these smelly pants all night. Two, you can take them off, and I'll wash them. Or three — ' she glanced at the scissors on the table ' — I can cut out the stain.'

'Cut it out then. Because I'm not taking off my pants.'

She lifted a shoulder. 'I don't know, Alex. It'll look better for Royce if you take them off.'

'Nikki . . . ' Alex's voice smoothed as if he were trying to reason with a small child. 'I'm in a vulnerable position here. Don't make this any harder on me than it has to be. The only way I'll remove my pants is if you let me stay untied afterward. If you want me to take them off so you can strap me back onto this chair wearing nothing but my shirt, socks, and boxers, my answer is no. I'd rather go with the cutting.'

Boxers, huh? That sounded so history-professor-ish. Dependable. Reliable.

So Alex.

A warm-honey feeling flowed through her.

Concentrate.

'But I have to keep you tied,' she explained. 'I can't trust that you won't try leaving the first time my back is turned.' She wasn't a mistrusting person by nature — in fact, Karin always cautioned her that she trusted too easily — but Alex Hart brandished a Ph.D.-trained brain and a burning desire to thwart her. Whether he wore traditional boxers, snug boxer-briefs, or a polka-dotted banana-sling, she had no doubt he'd use his considerable intelligence to attempt to trick her.

Besides, she might have disabled the van but she hadn't yet checked the occupancy status of the neighboring cabins. She couldn't risk Alex getting away and locating help.

'It's raining now,' he said mildly. 'Where would I go in the rain?'

Good one. 'It was raining when you tried untying the knot.'

'The rain's falling harder now. And I have no shoes.'

Nikki glanced toward the open cabin door as Santos tromped in with flecks of damp earth clinging to his paws. A sprinkle still fell, nothing more.

'Hardly Noah's-Ark stuff, Alex. You tried taking off without shoes the first time. What's to stop you from doing so again?'

'I've reconsidered.'

'Uh-huh. More likely you think I've lost my marbles. Not that I blame you, considering the circumstances. If I were you, I'd try running away from me, too.' She folded the damp tea towel and positioned it under the rear legs of the chair. Traction!

Remaining crouched, she gripped Alex's closest leg with one hand and the chair back with the other. Her chin grazed his shoulder. The earthy notes of his woody aftershave tickled her nostrils. *Nice.*

Royce often boasted that his expensive body spray smelled like money, which she found crass — both in description and aroma. She'd never succeeded in convincing him to switch to a subtler scent.

'I'm going to lift you up,' she informed Alex. 'If you help by leaning forward, I'll untie your hands for dinner. Or you can lie here and I'll feed you like a baby.'

A sigh trickled out of him. 'I'll try.'

She'd broken his spirit. Excellent. He'd be easier to handle from here on in.

'All right, here goes.' Straining like a weightlifter, she grunted, yarded, lugged, and hoisted Alex upright. Her muscles burned. She rolled her shoulders and stretched her spine. The gym membership her roommates had given her for her last birthday had come in handy. 'Thanks for helping.' She patted his shoulder. 'I'll reward you for your efforts. Until it's time to eat, though, I'm not taking the risk. I need to fix that knot.'

'I'm putty in your hands.'

She smiled. Amazing what the promise of a good meal could do.

She stepped behind the chair and refastened the knot, then brought in the supplies and laptop case. She closed the door.

Rusty wailed from inside the pet carrier. Santos curled up on the floor at the foot of one bed while Bernie yapped at the moose head.

Nikki shushed the dog.

She freed the cat and assembled the covered litter box. After placing the box in a corner, she fetched the scissors and returned to Alex.

'Sit as still as you can. I don't want to nick you.' Carefully, she clipped a path around the Bernie-christened fabric.

A ragged hole the size of her hand remained, exposing Alex's hair-dusted thigh . . . and a hint of gray flannel.

The boxers.

'Hmm.' She studied the hole. 'We'll pretend you spilled sauce on your pants.' She glanced up, meeting his gaze. 'For when Royce arrives.'

Alex's hazel eyes shadowed. 'Nikki, have you considered that he might not come?'

'Well, yeah, he might not come *tonight*. Not if he gets mad at me when he finds the note. But he'll be here tomorrow.' Holding the patch of wet fabric, she picked up the tea towel, rag, and crumpled duct tape.

'That's not what I meant. Have you entertained the idea that he might not come at all?'

Nikki frowned. 'How can you say that? Of course he'll come. He loves me.'

Does he?

Stupid inner voice!

She squeezed the wadded tape. She'd always believed in the power of love, the same strong love her grandparents had shared, the forever type of love her parents should share, yet didn't.

She squared her shoulders. She'd follow her grandparents' example. If genetic traits could skip generations, then, by God, the makeup of a marriage could, too.

Fie on Alex Hart for compelling her to consider otherwise. And to think she'd brought along a jar of homemade spaghetti sauce to serve him. He'd be lucky now if she slopped a tin of ancient sardines onto his plate.

4

Foiled Again

'How's your headache?'

Alex stopped stuffing his face with his second plateful of the best spaghetti and marinara sauce any man this side of Italy had surely tasted. He glanced at his abductor, who sat across the small table. 'Better, thanks to the ibuprofen.' He twirled a forkful of pasta. 'Nikki, this is *great*.'

A wide smile brightened her face. 'Thanks. I was out of sardines.' She pushed aside her empty plate, then laced her fingers on the table and leaned forward, watching him.

Always watching.

The woman possessed buckets of determination — not to mention the patience of a seasoned bride-in-waiting. Alex suspected that if Royce had it his way, she'd acquire a ton more experience in the patience department before she dragged Royce Carmichael to the altar.

But then Nikki St. James was a force to reckon with in her own right. Stubborn, illogical, a tad the far side of desperate. And cuter than any kidnapper Alex had ever read about.

Royce might be surprised to discover the lengths his fiancée would go to in pursuit of her goals. That was, if Royce bought this nutty setup and came after her.

Alex was surprised, at any rate. More than surprised. Begrudgingly impressed.

However harebrained Nikki's strategy, she believed in herself and her plan, which was more than he could say for himself these days.

'Sardines?' he echoed, lifting the spaghetti-wound fork to his mouth. Who put sardines in spaghetti? He chewed and swallowed. *Yum.* 'Never mind.'

So what if he couldn't figure out

what she meant? Rather than hounding her for a translation, like he would have a few hours ago, he let the oddball comment slide. After all, she had untied his hands for dinner, allowing him to toddle, the chair strapped to his butt, to the table. Her spaghetti sauce almost made up for the physical discomforts he'd endured.

He tore off a piece of garlic toast. As the crispy layers met his tongue, he groaned.

'You like?' Nikki asked.

'Oh yeah.' He ate the remaining chunk of toast, then resumed his inhalation of spaghetti. His hunger pangs receded.

Funny how starvation forced a man to re-examine his priorities. Or how a stomach filled with homemade chow enabled a guy to achieve a formerly elusive clarity of mind.

Sure, initially the negative aspects of the kidnapping had clouded his brain to the wisest — if truth be told, the only — course of action available to him.

But he definitely saw that course of action now.

Earlier, he'd been a fool to try escaping from Nikki and her merry band of misfits. He'd achieved nothing but a near-concussion and her eagle-eye on him every second.

A gorgeous eagle-eye, true, but an eagle-eye nonetheless.

The Nikki he'd come to know over the last several hours would never drop this latest jail-guard routine she had going unless she felt she could trust him. How would he earn that trust if he attempted to flee every time she left the room?

The key to gaining his freedom lay in proving his cooperation — and thereby lulling her into complacency.

Picking up his wooden salad bowl rubbed with spicy oil, he pierced the last tomato wedge with his fork.

'More salad?' she queried, and he nodded.

'Plus more of your homemade dressing, please. Thanks.' He flashed an appreciative smile.

'Coming right up.' She carried his bowl to the kitchen, the dogs trailing her.

That's it. Alex tracked her movements. *The more slack you give me, the better.*

But no midnight departure resided on his agenda. No struggling to reason with a desperately determined Nikki. He'd act the model prisoner and agree to whatever she'd planned for tonight. Guilt her into bestowing him her trust and, with it, the run of the cabin. He'd bide his time until daylight, play on that conscience she claimed to own, then make good on his escape tomorrow.

After breakfast.

★   ★   ★

Nikki leaned against the pillows on the springy double bed. Rusty had coiled into a ball on the worn peach comforter adorning her lap, while Bernie, exhausted from yipping at Murray the moose head, rested at her feet. Santos slumbered on the floor in a chasing-rabbits position.

She pushed up her nightgown sleeve and leafed through a magazine she'd brought along to pass the time. The candle jutting from an old wine bottle flickered on the nightstand between her bed and Alex's. The flame washed the glossy magazine pages in a muted glow that hopefully wouldn't disturb his sleep.

Yawning, she glanced over at her snoozing guest.

Her compliant and exceedingly cooperative guest.

She shook her head at the radical change in his behavior. Gram had always assured her that the road to a man's submission drove straight through his stomach, but Alex Hart had spun a total one-eighty since dinner. Her marinara sauce wasn't *that* good, so what was he trying to pull? Could she believe he'd decided to stick to her plan? That he wouldn't try running off again before Royce arrived?

Judging by how he'd allowed her to shackle him to the bedpost with the fur-lined handcuffs she'd . . . borrowed from one of her roommates, a lesser woman might say she could.

Yet . . .

She narrowed her gaze at his quilt-covered body. She'd handcuffed only his right wrist, for comfort, and his arm angled up toward the bedpost. His left arm slung across his middle, on top of the bedclothes. While he'd agreed to remove his belt and shirt — revealing an eyeful of sculpted chest that had jetted her pulse into the stratosphere — he'd insisted on wearing the mangled khakis to bed. The latter choice provided a major clue that, despite his apparently peaceful sleep, his crafty professor's mind could be devising new ways to foil her.

Even with the guy dead to the world, she couldn't quite trust him. He was too intelligent and complex, not little-boy charming like Royce.

Plus, she didn't love Alex like she did

Royce. She barely knew him.

What if, once she fell asleep, he awoke and broke free of the handcuffs? She couldn't count on Bernie's barking to alert her. The bushed pupster snoozed as soundly as Alex. And she couldn't keep her eyes glued to the man's . . . passable physique all night, or she'd sport bags the size of Seattle come morning. Not a pretty sight with which to greet her fiancé.

She chewed her lip. Alex's candlelit features had slackened with sleep, and two a.m. stubble roughened his jaw. His mouth — strong and sensual now that she thought about it — lifted at one corner, as if he were enjoying a particularly pleasant dream. His chin boasted a small, puckered scar.

She looked closer. A rather captivating scar it was, too. Like that of a rugged high-plains drifter, a man of the wilds, or a man of the wind. A rogue, an adventurer, a pirate —

A dizzying rush swept through her, and she blinked. The 'Sexiest Men of the Year' article she'd been skimming had provided ample fodder for her fertile imagination.

Tossing aside the magazine, she fought another yawn. If she wanted to get any sleep tonight, she had to stop thinking in mindless circles and *do* something. Not only something that would restrict Alex to the cabin tonight, but something that would prove as effective come morning. She was a woman of action now. No more Little Miss Passive.

Flinging back the comforter, she flounced out of bed. Rusty meowed and tumbled off her lap. She petted the cat until he settled again. Then she glanced at Alex.

Still asleep. Perfect.

She padded through the dark cabin.

Her weapon of choice lay in the kitchen.

★　★　★

'Wroof! Rif-rif-rif-rif-wroof! Rwrruff-wroof! Grrr . . . '

Alex's eyes popped open. The tortuous dreams of thirteenth-century stretching racks and daggers skipping over his abdomen crumbled beneath the reality of the mosquito-on-stilts atop his bare chest. Chihuahua eyeballs bulged, thin lips skinning back, tiny teeth bared — and zeroing in on his nose.

He jerked up.

Fiery pain gripped his wrist, and his head ricocheted back onto the pillow. *Agh*, the damn handcuffs!

He shielded his nose with his free hand. The devil-dog yelped, paws scrambling.

'Nikk-iiiii!' Alex clenched his jaw as Bernie the Barbarian bolted. The little dog soared from one bed to the other with the agility of a stuntman jumping rooftops. The cat awoke with a wail and dashed beneath Nikki's bed.

Nikki's footsteps sounded on the plank floor. Seconds later, her pretty face loomed over him.

'You bellowed?' she asked in her melodic voice. Behind her, Santos wedged between the beds. His hairy tail whapped Alex's mattress, and dust motes speckled the morning sun streaming through half-open curtains.

'Damn right I did. Your mutt seems to think I need rhinoplasty!'

Nikki glanced at Bernie now yipping on her bed. 'I was in the kitchen. I didn't see anything. What happened?'

'He tried *to bite off* my nose.' Alex tugged against the fur-lined handcuffs. 'Remove these so I can kill him.'

'You'll do no such thing!' Looking at Bernie again, she scolded the dog, 'Time for another session with the animal psychologist, I see. Fella, you're keeping me in the poorhouse. Why can't you and Alex get along?'

Bernie whined.

'Uh-uh, boy. Not this time. To the kitchen.' She pointed. 'I put out your food.'

The dog's ears pricked. Yipping, he flew off the bed.

Alex's captor stepped closer and studied his nose. Santos shoved in beside her leg. As the Saint Bernard gazed at Alex with rheumy eyes, his big tongue lolled . . . and dripped.

'No harm done,' Nikki said, tapping Alex's nose. She withdrew the handcuff key from a pocket of her white jeans. 'See this?' She dangled the miniscule object out of reach. 'The key to your freedom, Alex. But first I need your solemn promise as a history professor that you won't harm one hair on poor Bernie's head.'

'Poor *Bernie?*'

'You heard me. Not one.'

Alex rolled his eyes. 'Can I break his legs, at least?'

'I think not.'

'Use his whiskers for dental floss?'

'No!'

'Well, then, considering you're holding all the keys, Nikki, I'd say we have a deal.'

'Good.' She inserted the key into the lock. 'I'm sorry about Bernie's bad attitude, by the way. I doubt he's upset with you, though. It's probably Murray.'

'Who?'

'The moose head.' Forehead furrowing, she wiggled the key. Her pale green T-shirt — the same soft shade as her earrings — clung to her small breasts. As she leaned over Alex, the T-shirt crept up her waist. A tiny, silver hoop winked from the delicate dip of her navel.

Sexual need shot through him, strong, hot, and yearning. Handcuffs, a beautiful blonde, the pierced belly button . . .

Oh baby.

Too bad Nikki St. James was engaged to another. And not to some anonymous schlep, either. But to Royce, the schlep. Royce, his old pal, the schlep.

'The moose head?' he echoed. He tore away his gaze from her waist, only to find himself eyeballing her breasts again. Plump, perky, and perfect. Sized just right to fill his palms.

He stared at the rafters. 'Why the hell would you name a moose head?'

'Why the hell wouldn't I?' She

returned her attention to the handcuffs. 'This cabin belonged to my grandparents. When my sister and I visited, we didn't always get along. Gillian was into playing with her fashion dolls while I liked digging for worms and tracking animals in the woods with Gramps. She and I rarely shared secrets. I would have loved to, but — ' Drawing in a breath, she shrugged. 'Instead, I shared my secrets with Murray. He needed a name for that.'

She continued fiddling with the handcuffs. 'When I was real little, I thought Murray's body extended beyond the cabin wall. Each summer Gramps told me it wasn't there, but I didn't believe him. I always had to check outside to see if Murray had grown a body between visits.' Her lips tilted. 'Maybe Bernie thinks the same thing. Maybe he thinks Murray is real, so he keeps barking at him. You happened to be in the way this time.'

Alex nodded. How could he argue with such screwy logic? Besides, he had

more pressing matters on his mind —
and on his wrist.

He wiggled his hand. 'Do you have
any clue when you might get me out of
these?'

'I'm working on it.' She blew at a
silvery-blonde curl that had tumbled
onto her forehead. 'But something's
wrong. Wait, I see.' She examined the
handcuffs. 'I have to move a switch
before the key will work.'

'You mean you've never used these
before?'

She shook her head. 'They belong to
one of my roommates.'

'Ah.' So Nikki and Royce had never
shackled each other, huh? That knowledge shouldn't comfort Alex, but it
did.

'Not that I want to give you the
wrong idea about Lani,' Nikki said.
'Her sister, my other roommate, bought
her the handcuffs on a lark.'

Alex shrugged his free shoulder.
Whatever this Lani did in the privacy of
her bedroom was none of his business.

However, neither were Nikki's sexual escapades.

He must remember that.

Nikki thumbed the switch on the handcuff and tried the key again. *Click.* Music to his ears.

The handcuff fell away, and he lowered his aching arm. 'Thanks.' He rubbed his stiff right shoulder and then his wrist. A red impression marked the skin, but the fur lining had prevented the metal cuff from biting deep.

All in all, he'd survive. Agreeing to the overnight shackling was a small price to pay toward encouraging Nikki to trust him long enough to achieve his escape.

'Can I get up now? I need to use the outhouse.' He prided himself on his reasonable tone.

'I'll take you in a minute. The fridge is open. I should close it first.' Leaving the handcuff dangling from the bedpost, she backed up between the beds with Santos. As the Saint Bernard ambled toward the couch, the cat peeked from beneath the second bed and Bernie trotted out of the kitchen.

'What time is it?' Alex flexed his sore shoulder.

'Eight-thirty.' Nikki turned away. 'I'm making Denver omelets,' she said without looking back. 'We might have an hour or two before Royce arrives. No sense starving.'

'An omelet sounds great.' Alex's stomach rumbled. If Nikki made eggs with the same gourmet flair as her spaghetti sauce, then he was in kidnapping heaven.

He threw aside the quilt. Cool air wafted over his legs, and khaki strips fluttered.

Forget the eggs! What had happened to his pants?

Last night, she'd cut a hole in the fabric. But now —

The material was shredded from mid-thigh down, as if a rabid grizzly had ripped sharp claws through the cloth. Or a demented blonde armed with a pair of rusty scissors had assaulted them.

'Nikk-*iiiiii!*' He sprang out of the bed. The fronts of his pants hung from his legs in wide ribbons. He swatted a hand behind himself, grazing his rump. Thank God the backs hadn't met the same fate. '*What* were you thinking?'

What if he'd awoken mid-snip? One startled move and . . . instant vasectomy. He shuddered.

She pushed a hand through her curls and faced him. 'You noticed.'

'I'd have to be dead not to notice! Why would you do this?'

'Really, Alex, you're blustering like a bull in heat. All that anger isn't good for your digestion. Besides, you're scaring Bernie.' She scooped the whining dog into her arms. 'You don't want me to tie you to the chair again, do you? Or slap on the handcuffs until Royce arrives? I had to find some way to keep you here.'

Her gaze drifted over him, and she smiled. Calm, collected, and infuriating. 'I guess you could try leaving, anyway, dressed like that. But I have every confidence that you won't get far.

We're miles from the highway, and no driver in his right mind would pick you up. Sorry, Alex, but you don't look very history professor-ish right now. You kinda look like a deranged superhero. You know that huge green guy with the amazing pecs who pops out of his clothes whenever he blows his top? Except his pants are purple.'

Alex flung up his hands. 'What did you expect? That I'd take the demolition of my clothes lying down?'

'Well, actually, you *were* — '

'Don't say it!' He stalked to the toilet-less bathroom and slammed the door. Knuckles rigid, he gripped the sink. His heart pounded like it might catapult out of his heaving chest. He grabbed the toothbrush the lunatic blonde had provided and scoured his teeth until his gums ached.

After punishing his face in a similar ritual with the washcloth, he stomped back into the main room. Nikki remained standing, cradling the psychotic Bernie. The damn dog growled from the safety of her embrace.

'Shh.' She scratched the mosquito's ears.

Alex searched the messy quilt on his bed. All he found were the dog-chewed socks.

He sat on the saggy mattress and yanked them on. 'Where's my shirt?'

Her gaze wavered. 'Um . . . '

'My shirt,' he repeated. 'I left it on the bottom of the bed last night. Now it's gone. Where is it?'

'Woof?' Santos seconded from beside the couch.

Nikki stroked Bernie. 'How should I phrase this?' She paused. 'Last night, after you fell asleep, I noticed your shirt had . . . taken on a certain aroma. A quasi-canine quality, shall we say. And none too pleasant, let me tell you.'

Alex snorted. 'After the way Santos slobbered all over me in the van, I don't doubt it. That's the only shirt I have, Nikki. I want it.' He stood.

'Well, that's a problem.'

'Why?'

'Because I . . . ' *mumble, mumble* ' . . . in the outhouse.'

His spine seized. 'You put my shirt in the outhouse?'

'Woof!'

'Make that down the outhouse.'

'*Down* the outhouse?'

'Woof!'

'Well, it stunk.'

'You threw my shirt down the outhouse?' He thumped the bases of both hands against his skull. 'What kind of twisted kidnapper are you? My cell phone and laptop better not be down there!'

'Don't be daft.' Bernie squirmed in her arms, and she deposited the mutt onto the floor. The Chihuahua dashed to the bed Rusty lurked beneath. A feline paw swiped out, and Bernie danced back. 'Karin has your electronics. She'll keep them safe. And I'll buy you another shirt to go along with the new pants I promised,' she stated as if the solution were obvious. 'In fact, once Royce and I return to Seattle, I'll buy however many shirts you need.' She scanned his naked chest. 'What's your size?'

Alex clenched his fists. Royce again. The woman had enough faith to part the Red Sea, and she'd placed it all in a guy who cared more about her society connections than the hallowed state of matrimony she coveted.

'Forget the shirt,' he muttered. 'Give me the keys to your van.'

'They won't do you any good.'

'They'll do me plenty of good, I assure you.' Like getting him away from this wacky woman and back to his staid, predictable life.

'All right, if you insist. They're on the kitchen counter.'

He strode to the kitchen and snatched the keys. The tattered pants slapping his legs, he stomped out of the cabin.

The ground had softened from last night's rain, and dirt clung to the soles of his socks. His loafers were in the van somewhere — unless she'd tossed them in the outhouse, too.

He wouldn't waste another second finding out.

Climbing into the van, he jammed the key in the ignition.

Nothing.

He turned the key again. S.O.L. The damn engine was dead.

Grinding his teeth, he tromped back into the cabin. Nikki stood at the kitchen counter, humming and chopping green peppers. The animals lounged in the main room, in various stages of grooming and napping.

'The van won't start.'

'I know,' she replied without pausing in her task.

His teeth wore down another inch. 'Would you also happen to know why?'

Still chopping, she smiled. 'I misplaced the distributor cap.'

He counted to three. *Patience, Hart. She WANTS to drive you nuts.*

'Where is it?'

'Alex, I'm not going to *tell* you.' She glanced up. 'Telling you would defeat the purpose behind hiding it.'

Of course. How silly of him.

Frustration was too mild a word for the emotion throttling his neck. He had no clothes, no transportation, not a clue where they were. He didn't know when Royce would arrive, or even if the jerk would come. Meanwhile, Nikki refused to spare him an ounce of pity.

So much for gaining her trust. He couldn't even win her compassion. The revenge demon inside him would love nothing better than to hog-tie and handcuff her in the outhouse with that schizophrenic yapper, slobbering mammoth, and spitting feline for the next two thousand years — and see how *she* liked it.

But retribution wasn't the answer. He couldn't reduce himself to strong-arm tactics with this woman. Somehow, he had to outsmart her. Or put her off-balance.

Or both.

'Fair enough.' He tossed the keys onto the counter. 'But if you think I'm parading around in this getup, you're mistaken.' He tugged off the muddy socks. 'I'm wearing so few clothes as it is, I might as well strip nude. The Garden-of-Eden look will convince Royce we're about to have sex better than the hulking green guy, anyway.' He reached for his zipper. 'That's the effect you're going for, right?'

'No!' The butcher knife clattered to the counter. 'I mean, yes, I want Royce to suspect us. But you don't need to strip, Alex. At least not right now. And definitely not all the way.'

'That's a switch. Last night, you said I should take off my pants.'

'Your pants, not your boxers!' Her hands flitted like startled humming-birds. 'The stripping isn't necessary. We'll wait until we hear Royce's car, then jump into bed and pretend we're just starting.'

'Just starting what?' He stared at her. 'Spell it out, Nikki. I'm fairly dense.'

'M-making love.'

'Terrific. I get it now. Why wait?' He

stepped toward her. 'We have to get this right, Nik, or my old buddy Royce won't buy it. When he barges in, we can't waste time giving each other innocent pecks on the cheek. We'll need to feel at home swapping spit.' Grasping her upper arms, he lowered his mouth to hers. Her lips parted on a gasp, and her warm, sweet breath filled his mouth.

So sweet.

Need pumping, he deepened the kiss. Nikki moaned. *Oh yeah.*

Cupping her face, he coaxed her tongue to meet his. A moment later, their tongues twisted, and his excitement stirred.

'Woof!'

Nikki's hands clamped his wrists, clutching him closer before pushing him away. 'A-A-Alex.' Her eyes were wide, her mouth wet, and her cheeks pink. 'I think I heard Royce. Did you?' She darted to the cabin door. Yanking it wide, she stuck her head outside. 'Royce?'

Alex grunted. *Royce. Again.* Who was she trying to kid? Santos had wandered into the kitchen. The old dog's bark was deep, but easily distinguishable from the rumble of Royce's flashy sports car.

Obviously, Nikki had grabbed at any excuse to pull away from him.

In contrast, *his* arousal was readily apparent. Hardly an appropriate reaction, considering his best-man status.

Way to go, Hart.

While her back was turned, he visualized Bernie about to make mincemeat out of him. By the time Nikki closed the door, a respectable air of normality had been assumed.

Clearing her throat, she faced him. 'It wasn't Royce.'

No duh. 'Santos barked.'

'He did? Um, in that case, thanks for the, uh, lip-lock, Alex. We don't need to try it again.'

'Once was enough, huh?'

'More than enough.' She glanced away. 'Not that the kiss wasn't adequate for our purposes. It was . . . more than adequate. It was — *ahem*

— quite enough.'

Gee, thanks. What every guy wants to hear.

He jerked a thumb toward his Robinson-crucified pants. 'Glad to oblige, Nik, but there's still the issue of my clothes. It's not exactly ninety degrees in this place, and I feel and look ridiculous.'

'But I *want* you to look ridiculous. So you won't run off.'

'Yeah, I get that. Is there any way you can achieve your objective without giving me pneumonia?'

She bit a thumbnail. 'I don't think so.'

'Then they're coming off.' He fished a hand toward the waistband.

Nikki squeaked. 'But you can't!'

'Yes, I can.'

'But you *won't*.'

'Yeah, I will.' He popped the button.

'Alex!' She clapped her hands to cherry-stained cheeks. 'You wouldn't dare!'

He unzipped. 'Try me.'

5

Now or Never

'We're bound to find something in here that will fit you . . . sort of,' Nikki assured Alex as she dug through the cardboard box marked 'Clothes' among the storage items flanking the back door. He'd crouched beside her in the tattered khakis, invading her space and her peace of mind. Her pulse raced from the aftershocks of his near-striptease and her lips hadn't stopped sizzling since he'd kissed her.

Thank Cupid he'd zipped his pants again when she'd shrieked and squeezed shut her eyes. Aside from a fumbling college experience that hadn't resulted in going all the way, Royce was the only man she'd ever seen nude — and that was how it should be. Alex wearing traditional boxers she could *maybe* handle, but Alex strutting around as naked as Adam pushed the illusion that they were lovers too far.

'Gramps was only five-eight and . . . rotund, if you know what I mean,' she said as Rusty meowed and rubbed his whiskered face against the cardboard box. A few feet away, Bernie gnawed one of Alex's socks while Santos sniffed the storage items. 'If you wear his clothes, you'll feel plenty warm, yet still look ridiculous. Then we'll both be happy.' She handed over two mothball-scented garments. 'Try these.'

Grumbling, Alex eyed the orange plaid work shirt and scruffy brown polyester pants.

Nikki raised her chin. 'Beggars can't be picky, Alex. Those were Gramps's favorite fishing clothes. If they were good enough for him, they're good enough for you.' Besides, the ill-fitting outfit would lend the handsome professor a disreputable look certain to put off any driver considering picking up a hitchhiker. Too bad she hadn't thought of searching the storage boxes before she'd altered Alex's wardrobe.

'Choosers,' he stated grimly. 'Beggars can't be *choosers*.'

'And they can't afford to be picky, either. Honestly, Alex, I never pegged you for such a grump.'

His eyebrows webbed. 'A grump?'

'You heard me.' Lifting Rusty into her arms, she stood. 'So I kidnapped you — it's not for long. So I tied you up — you survived. I feel guilty enough about putting you through this whole ordeal without you pouring salt in my wounds.' She petted the squirming cat until his ears flattened.

Clutching the garments, Alex rose. 'If you feel guilty, why not let me leave?'

'You *know* why. I need you here. I thought you understood that. I need you to help me show Royce how serious I am about making a commitment. A wedding date, not just a ring. That he'll risk losing me if he doesn't.' She tightened her grip on Rusty, and the glitzy engagement ring twisted on her finger. The extravagant setting bit into her pinky. 'Any fool can give a woman a ring. It takes a man of honor to honor his commitments.'

Her stomach clenched. *Was* Royce a man of honor? Or was he a fool? If this weekend pointed to the latter, then didn't that make *her* double the dunderhead for believing in him all this time?

'A fool and his fiancée are soon parted, Alex. If Royce doesn't come after me — if he doesn't fight to keep me — then I'll know we aren't meant to stay together.' Her eyes stung. Closing them against sudden tears, she swallowed. 'Now I'm sorry about the sad state of my grandfather's clothes. I'm sorry about everything. But I'm doing the best I can, Alex. If you can't bring yourself to help me, please tell me now.' She opened her eyes. Rusty hung over her arm, mewling like a terrified kitten. Bernie abandoned the sock and trotted over to join her. Santos bordered her on the right, his hefty bulk comforting as he panted.

And Alex . . . the poor guy just stood there, holding the fishing clothes, an advertisement for flabbergasted.

Her cheeks heated. 'Oh Alex, I'm sorry for dumping all over you. That was uncalled for. That was — '

'It's okay,' he murmured. 'I'll wear the clothes, Nikki.'

'You will?'

He nodded. 'Royce obviously means more to you than I realized, or . . . ' his jaw worked ' . . . perhaps more than I wanted to believe. I don't want to see you hurt, Nik. And I hope to hell that Royce doesn't, either.'

'Of course he doesn't want to see me hurt. He loves me.' Her voice squeaked.

Great. Where was her confidence?

Sucking in a breath, she avoided Alex's gaze. She didn't want to see the doubt in his eyes, didn't want to read the questions now plaguing her. *If Royce loves me, why isn't he here yet? Why didn't he drive up last night to get me?*

Considering the roundabout route she'd chosen to travel to the cabin, Alex might assume the trip from Seattle always took four hours. However, anyone half-capable of operating a GPS could reach Lake Eden in two.

And Royce was much more than capable.

Pain stabbed her heart — and then her arm. Wincing, she freed the cat claw hooking her skin.

Rusty jumped onto the floor. Tail flaring, he dashed beneath the nearest bed. Bernie, eyes bulging at Alex, left the cat alone for once. Santos continued panting.

'Royce *will* get here,' she said. 'Maybe he got a flat tire or had to stay overnight at a motel.' Maybe a problem had occurred with the ferries, and he'd needed to catch a later sailing. However, she couldn't voice that possibility without dropping Alex a clue about their location.

The professor shrugged. 'It's possible.'

'The point is, Royce will come. And soon. He will come soon.' Listen to her, repeating herself. Who needed convincing, Alex or *her?* That she possessed any qualms about the man she planned to marry —

She slammed the brakes on her traitorous thoughts. She *had* to believe in Royce's love for her, in their love for each other. She wanted a marriage built on faith and trust. If she couldn't trust that Royce would come for her after reading the anxious undertones of her note, her entire plan was doomed.

Another idea occurred, and she blinked. *Two* ideas occurred, and they kept getting worse!

What if her plan backfired and Royce didn't come, not because he didn't love her, but because he'd missed the note somehow, or . . . or the thought of her hooking up with Alex hurt him so much that he left her?

Yikes. Had she made a colossal mistake?

Cold marbles scrambled around in

her chest. She firmed her mouth. No, she couldn't have botched this weekend so thoroughly. Royce *would* arrive to stop her from having a fictional fling with Alex. To believe anything else placed her faith in her fiancé — and their entire future — at risk.

Her worry must have shown on her face, because Alex stepped closer, concern all over his. Bernie stiffened to full alert, his soprano growl reverberating in the quiet morning. Alex ignored the dog's posturing. His gaze, his attention, remained focused on her.

'Hey,' he said softly, shifting the musty clothes from one arm to the other. 'Whatever you believe about Royce is fine by me.'

The acidic scent of mothballs lingered between them, but didn't have a hope of distracting her from his nearness, his solid, dependable presence.

He stood . . . so close. So big and masculine and half-dressed.

Her heart thumped. 'You're not sure

Royce is even coming, are you?'

'Who am I to say? Just a stressed out kidnapping victim. You can't blame me for being a little on edge, Nikki.' A wry smile touched his mouth. 'You love Royce. You want to marry him. That's enough for me.' He paused. 'Royce wants to marry you, too, Nik. I know he does. He's told me.'

The invisible fist gripping her heart loosened. 'He has?'

Alex nodded. 'I'm his best man. It's my job to know these things. If you want to marry Royce, it will happen.' His gaze drifted over her. 'When the day comes, I'll do my part as best man. I'll get him to the church on time, Nik. For you.'

His husky voice burrowed through her. Gold flecks radiated from his dark pupils and burnished the hazel irises to bronze. Something oddly akin to desire fluttered inside her as his gaze lowered to her mouth, then slowly back up.

Would he kiss her again?

For a positively pre-adulterous moment

— Cupid help her — she wanted him to.

He reached out a hand ... and brushed her cheek, his thumb pad rough and the trailing palm warm. His hand curved her face in a too-brief caress. His touch gentle but urgent. Barely there, yet branding. Yearning.

A whispery murmur escaped her. Heat flooded her, beckoning, churning.

Why this intense response to Alex? Why Alex, yet not with Royce — her only real lover?

Royce had never touched her with such compelling restraint. Could that be why? He'd always taken great care to be gentle, but a different sort of gentleness than she experienced with Alex.

Royce's touch carried a certain detachment that presumably signified his respect for her as his fiancée and future wife. He'd explained his reasoning in tender tones the few times she'd brought up their infrequent lovemaking.

Eventually, not wanting to come across like some sex fiend, she'd stopped asking.

Sometimes she wished her fiancé didn't respect her so damn much.

'G-Gramps's clothes.' She touched the folded garments Alex held. 'I'll air them out while you're in the shower. You'd like a shower before breakfast, right?'

'Yeah,' he replied in a gravelly tone. 'Preferably freezing.'

Her pulse jumped. 'Perfect, because the water tank isn't very big, and I think I used all the hot while you were asleep. Sorry.' She took the clothes. 'Maybe you'll get lucky — um, maybe the water's warm again.'

His gaze smoldered. 'I'm sure it's the temperature I need.' He disappeared into the bathroom.

The door closed, and she released a breath.

Phew! Talk about tension. Thick and rich and warm — like gooey butter-scotch. And every bit as tempting.

131

No. Even more so.

Her heart raced. *Be still, darn you.* She knew precisely what was going on here. She'd watched enough reality TV dating shows and had read enough relationship e-zines to understand the phenomenon arising between her and Alex. Place a man and woman alone in close quarters and proximity played clever tricks on the libido. It didn't mean anything. It could happen to anyone. That it had never before happened to her was a detail she shouldn't worry about. An oddity she should ignore.

Good plan.

She strode to the back door with the musty clothes, the dogs accompanying her. As she passed the bathroom, the tinkling of water from the ancient showerhead echoed off the metal stall walls.

By now, Alex would have stripped nude to stand beneath the water's spray, his muscular chest boasting a sheen of frothy soap bubbles, his strong thighs planted apart and dripping water, his —

Oh my. How yummy.

Her tummy knotted. *Stop that!*

If any fantasizing occurred this morning, her hot daydreams would feature Royce. Royce, who was traveling this very minute to come claim her.

Royce, the man who loved her and would soon prove it. Her one and only. Her future hubby.

No more thoughts of Alex, only Royce.

The shower water thrumming in her ears, she dashed outside.

RoyceRoyceRoyceRoyceRoyce.

* * *

What the hell was wrong with him?

Lukewarm water spurted from the tiny showerhead and over Alex's scalp. He pressed his palms against the metal shower wall, shoulders and thigh muscles bunched. He wasn't fifteen years old! *Control yourself.*

He had Nikki to thank for the odd cocktail of lust and remorse. Between her imaginative antics and her angelic blue eyes, she'd turned his body, mind, and his damn structured world inside out.

In less than twenty-four hours, too — a personal record.

He'd never met a woman who affected him the way Nikki did. Who frustrated and irritated him even while he wanted her all to himself.

And wasn't that the joke of it?

He'd never burned for another guy's woman — not like this. Hadn't considered himself capable of any form of cheating. However, when he'd touched Nikki's face minutes ago, the urge to pull her into his arms had swelled in his chest like a nuclear mushroom cloud. Instant and danger-ous. Overwhelming. Spurred not solely from the desire to kiss her again — although, oh yeah, he'd wanted to do that — but also from a crazy need to protect her.

From her naïveté.

From potential heartache.

But, most of all, from Royce.

He sluiced cooling water through his hair. *What a drip*. After the countless times he'd unintentionally mucked up his sisters' love lives with his over-protective big-brother routine, he should have learned to cultivate some finesse. But no. Example: moments ago with Nikki, he'd had no right to insinuate that Royce was quite willing to hurt her. That the schlep might not play into her romantic fantasy and race to the cabin to 'rescue' her like the man of honor she desperately wanted to see him as.

At least he'd had the decency to back off when he'd caught the flash of pain in her eyes. But the damage was done. He'd placed doubt in her mind when he had no idea what Royce would do. All he had were his suspicions to the contrary, based on his undergrad years of witnessing Royce 'The Hound' Carmichael in chick-manipulating action. The guy's bragging about Nikki's acceptance of his sexual needs also pointed to a no-show.

In all probability, Royce had seen through Nikki's scheme from the start and hadn't bought the threat of a hookup at all. Sure, the jerk *might* do right by his fiancée and arrive at the cabin eventually, like in a couple of days. Probably after taking advantage of Nikki's absence to fool around. To Royce's way of thinking, a late appearance would allow him to have his fun while stringing her along until he won the true love of his life — the partnership in her father's dermatology practice.

Major points scored for The Hound in that scenario, but what about Nikki?

The shower water chilled, and Alex gritted his teeth. If he left before his old college roommate arrived, Nikki's world would shatter. And, while he'd been careful not to agree to help her, her ploy would crumble without him.

To top it off, she wouldn't have a soul to turn to if Alex vamoosed and then Royce didn't appear. No one but her dogs to lean on — and Bernie was a mite too short for that.

She'd be alone. Upset. Heartbroken. Needy.

She would need *someone*.

He needed to decide if that someone would be him.

*   *   *

Is It Lust Or Love?

Nikki allowed her pen to hover over the multiple-choice quiz in the women's magazine open on the kitchen counter. Her gaze skipped to question three — that most perplexing of issues:

When he kisses you, do you . . . ?

(A) *Shoot off like Fourth of July fireworks?*
(B) *Sizzle like a Halloween sparkler?*
(C) *Fizzle like a dud?*

In Alex's case, definitely A.

Squirming, she circled the letter and scribbled Alex's initial beside it. As for Royce . . . she sighed . . . her fiancé's kisses had always registered between C and B. And lately C had reigned supreme — mucho aggravating.

Nibbling the pen cap, she looked over her shoulder. Alex sat at the table with Santos at his feet, while Bernie yapped at Murray and Rusty chased an invisible mouse. Whistling, Alex arranged the battered Monopoly game in preparation for the tournament Nikki had suggested. Her grandfather's clothes hung absurdly loose on him, but he hadn't complained about the fit since *her* little fit by the storage boxes. However, whenever she cast a surreptitious glance his way, she'd glimpse tension in the narrowing of his eyes or the stiffness of his torso. Then he'd notice her watching him, and his demeanor would change, soften and relax. Like this weird addition of the cheerful whistling. Except it sounded oddly off. As if he were faking it.

But who faked whistling?

She gnawed the pen. Was Alex obsessing about their kiss like she was? Did he feel the same disloyalty toward Royce that balled like tiny fists in her chest and whipped confusion through her veins?

Her gnawing progressed to chomping, and the pen cap cracked.

Grow up, Nikki.

She returned her attention to the lust quiz. Moments later, she groaned. There was no way around it — her 'Alex' answers simply must equal lust! She'd awarded the man far too many A's than was reasonable. Therefore, her physical response to him *wasn't* reasonable. Certainly nothing as romantic and enduring as love.

Inhaling, she flipped the pages to the quiz key.

'How's that lemonade coming?' Alex's voice boomed behind her.

She slapped shut the magazine and shoved it behind a canister. 'Ready.' She grabbed the glasses. *Right*.

She'd never felt less prepared for anything in her life.

* * *

Several hours and three Monopoly games later, Alex remained tangled in the throes of indecision.

On one hand, logic argued that any woman capable of continually buying the game's most profitable color groups and then building hotels on those properties faster than a business mogul on a construction spree possessed the fortitude to survive a fiancé no-show. On the other hand, Nikki's undying devotion to Royce reinforced his first impression of her as a girl who thought primarily with her heart and not her mind.

Could he abandon her to suffer a cruel life lesson alone?

'Want to play best out of five?' she asked from across the small table. She bit into an apple she'd fetched from the kitchen moments ago, following the ending of their third game. Her lips pressed against the bright red fruit as her perfect white teeth sunk home.

He shook his head. 'No, thanks.' Averting his gaze from her sexy mouth, he pushed back his chair. 'Losing three for three is enough battering for my ego.'

'What are you talking about? You won the second game.'

'Barely.' He'd managed to scrape up the win because Rusty had distracted her with his constant howling for food. The cat ate every thirty minutes. Not low-odor dry kibbles, either, but moist canned stuff that stunk worse than Santos's breath. Nikki had explained that the Siamese hoarded during the day so he could sleep uninterrupted at night. A likely story. Rusty needed the extra calories to fuel his maniac racing around the cabin whenever Bernie barked at the moose head. Which occurred irritatingly often.

Like right now.

141

A headache throbbed at the base of Alex's skull. He couldn't blame the pounding on his fall in the chair last night. His head only hurt when the puny mutt barked. All efforts to calm the hyper spitball had failed. Under Nikki's direction — as part of her campaign to convince Bernie that Murray didn't have a body and therefore posed no threat — Alex had removed the dusty moose head from the wall and propped it against the piano.

What an exercise in frustration. Bernie's frantic yipping had continued unabated, and Rusty's cabin-zooming had increased tenfold.

Even Santos had gotten into the act, slobbering his tongue over Murray's glass eyeballs before returning to sniff the storage boxes — and knocking three or four over.

The old dog now lay beneath the table, snoring in a canine coma after having licked Alex's toes that stuck out from his borrowed flip-flops.

How could the Saint Bernard sleep amid such chaos? How could *Nikki* endure this insanity?

'Doesn't that little mutt ever shut up?'

Her gaze widened. 'Watch it!'

Rusty leapt onto Alex's lap and across the table, scattering game pieces. Nikki shrieked and dropped her apple on Park Place as the cat sailed past Go. Paper play money danced in the air like confetti. With a blue fifty stuck to one paw, Rusty dashed into the kitchen.

Alex stood. 'That does it. Nikki, the moose head has to go. Bernie is becoming more freaked, not less, and I can't take it anymore.'

He strode to the piano and hoisted Murray. Nikki hurried after him. Dust puffed off the massive antlers, clogging his lungs. He coughed. Bernie growled at his feet.

'Where to?' he asked his blonde jailer.

'Do we have to? I hate to think of Murray — '

Alex grunted. '*Yes*.'

Her shoulders sagged. 'Darn it, you're right. As much as I love Murray, he's giving Bernie conniptions.'

'That's . . . ' *grunt* ' . . . putting it . . . ' *grunt* ' . . . mildly.'

'You can store him in the shed, I guess,' she chattered as if he held a paperweight, not a dead weight. 'Or maybe the van. Except Bernie likes to play in there sometimes — '

'So no van,' he interrupted. Damn it, Murray weighed a ton. What had the taxidermist stuffed him with? Cement?

'Where's this shed?' he asked between Bernie's barks.

'Out back. I'll show you.'

'No.'

'No?' Eyebrows arching, she propped a hand on one curvy hip. Her short T-shirt lifted, and the silver ring adorning her belly button glinted. 'Who's in charge here, anyway?'

'You are, Queen of Sheba.' Alex arched his spine to compensate for Murray's bulk. A dead fly slid off the antlers and bounced on his nose. He sneezed. 'You have to trust me sooner or later, though. I didn't run away when you walked the dogs after breakfast, did I?' Although he nearly had. His indecision over leaving her stranded had kept him caged. As had the fact that she'd locked him inside.

The windows hadn't been as easy to jimmy as he'd assumed when they'd first arrived. He knew because he'd tried. Regardless . . .

'If I'd wanted to, I could have broken a window to escape. I had motive, I had opportunity, and — ' he hefted Murray higher ' — I had means.'

She frowned. 'You would have thrown Murray through a window?'

'I *could* have. But I didn't.' She never would have forgiven him if he'd damaged Murray. 'What does that tell you?'

'You're trustworthy?'

He grunted.

'All right, you've proven yourself. But you're taking Santos with you, as a sentry. No arguments.'

'I wouldn't dream of it.' Yes, he would. How could he not? Freedom beckoned like a street-corner huckster. *Act fast! Buy now! Great deal! Just a little hot!* Escape was his for the taking.

Except you don't want to see Nikki hurt, remember?

Tension bunched in his neck.

Nikki woke Santos. Seconds later, the back door shut behind Alex and the dog. The serenity of the outdoors swept over him. *Ah . . .*

Amid the utter stillness of the mountain retreat, Nikki's voice carried from inside the cabin. She softly chastised Bernie and Rusty, meanwhile trusting *him* completely, it seemed.

Swearing, he headed for a weathered, vine-covered structure beside a horse-shoe pit choked with weeds. Santos trotted along. The May afternoon sun shone through wispy clouds in a sky as blue as Nikki's eyes. In contrast, the brisk air sat below seventy. The warm but baggy clothes cinched to his body by a pair of ancient suspenders would serve him well once evening descended.

The biceps of both arms burning, he lowered Murray into the tall grass between the shed and horseshoe area. Santos, apparently not well acquainted with the definition of 'sentry,' wandered into the heavy brush and hemlocks cramming the hillside.

Alex opened the shed door, and rusty hinges creaked. The mildewed scent of damp and decaying wood blew up his nostrils as he swept a hand along the wall for a light switch. No luck. A bare bulb and chain probably hung in the middle of the space.

As he slapped away sagging cobwebs, his moderately nearsighted eyes adjusted to the dim interior. He pushed aside a toolbox to make room for Murray —

And then he saw it . . . the key to a quick escape. Leaning against the wall like a gift from the kidnapping gods. Like the fickle finger of fortune pointing the way.

Heart pounding, he wrapped a hand

around the shabby pink frame and inspected the old kid's bike. A white basket drooped on the handlebars, but the chain remained intact and the seat felt sturdy beneath his palm. Too bad the tires were flat.

He dug through a pile of junk near the bike and located an old bike pump.

He inflated the front tire. He needed to seize this opportunity — now that it stared him in the face. Riding the bike would work better than running down the rutted road in spongy flip-flops. Better than wasting time knocking on cabin doors, hoping to find an occupant who'd believe his crazy story and help him.

He patted a pocket of the too-short pants. Nikki might have stolen his glasses, keys, cell, laptop, and computer case, but she'd neglected to frisk him for his wallet. He'd slept on the slim lump all night, then transferred the wallet to her grandfather's flood pants while changing clothes in the bathroom after his shower.

With his university ID vouching for his respectability, and his debit and credit cards paying his way, he'd rent a car in the nearest town, race back to Seattle, find Royce — and shake the guy by the lapels of his two-thousand-dollar suit until the zit doctor agreed to come after Nikki.

Hell, Alex would *drag* Royce to the cabin to get him to do right by his fiancée.

He pumped air into the rear tire. Tossing aside the pump, he straddled the bike and bounced his butt on the seat to test the wheels. His knees knocked the handlebars, but he'd survive. He climbed off the bike and walked it to the shed door.

He propped the little bike against an interior wall. He wasn't a complete ass. He'd store Murray in the shed as promised and *then* take off. Rattle Royce before returning to his own predictable routine. Dig into research for his academic paper, remain focused on tenure. Trying to relax for even one weekend had steered him miles off-track.

In the middle of nowhere with a sexy blonde he'd had no right kissing.

And no damn business wanting.

He slipped out of the shed and lifted Murray from the grass.

From somewhere behind the building, Santos yelped.

6

Never

Alex dumped Murray into the tall grass and darted toward the noise. Santos's yelps and howls devolved into anguished whining.

'Santos!' Damn, he should have kept the dog with him. Where was he? 'Santos!'

As Alex searched the area around the horseshoe pit, Nikki raced out of the cabin, Bernie yipping at her heels. The back door whacked shut behind them.

'What happened?' She glanced around. 'Where's Santos?'

'I don't know. I was in the shed, making room for Murray . . . ' Alex let his voice trail off. He wouldn't deliberately lie about his activities in the weathered shack, but he couldn't tell Nikki the truth, either. Worry filled her eyes for her cherished pet. They had to find him.

A second later, the dog crept out of the hillside brush, sporting a new set of whiskers.

'Santos!' Nikki's hands flew to her chest. 'My poor boy! He's been quilled!'

She ran to the dog, Bernie trailing her. Alex followed at a slower clip. Stupid flip-flops. Stupid *him*.

He hadn't considered that Santos might frighten a porcupine in the woods. For that matter, he hadn't considered that the dog might have stumbled across an old bear trap — or a pack of hungry coyotes. He'd thought only of his escape, nothing more.

He reached the Saint Bernard and the dog's angel-haired owner. A half-dozen porcupine quills sprouted from Santos's snout. Two more jutted from the dog's chin like a sparse goatee. The large animal shook his head. Whining, Santos flopped onto the ground and rubbed his dark nose.

Nikki crouched beside the dog and whispered soft, comforting words, her hands floating above her pet, as if she wanted to touch him but wasn't certain she should. Next to her, Bernie stood quietly.

Alex knelt on her other side, near Santos's head. The dog gazed at him with mournful eyes.

'Oh man. Sorry, boy.'

Nikki looked up. 'Why wasn't he with you?' She flicked her fingers. 'Never mind.' She returned her attention to the whining dog, stilling his paws with gentle caresses.

'Curiosity's supposed to kill the cat, not quill my fella,' she chided Santos gently. 'But you're always poking your nose into trouble, aren't you, boy? Well, it could have been worse. There are only a few quills. Think if Bernie had found that porky, huh? He'd look like a pupster pincushion.'

Bernie's tawny ears pricked, and he yipped. Nikki glanced at the smaller dog. 'Hush.'

She continued soothing Santos with silky tones while Alex watched. She was a total natural with animals. It was incredible, really. Her love and concern for her hurt pet shone through even as she took control. He'd expected copious tears, but she exuded a calm confidence. Efficiency underscored her caring for the moaning dog.

Man, he'd been dead wrong about Nikki. Yeah, she was a kooky piece of work at times, but hardly the ditzy party girl with a penchant for sex and sin Royce had described.

Alex hated it when people assumed they knew him based on his all-work-no-play reputation, yet he'd judged Nikki by similarly shallow standards. He had a lot to learn about reading others. For someone who'd once possessed the knack to pinpoint a student's strengths and weaknesses within the first few days of classes, that was a sobering conclusion.

Had he buried himself in the books too long? His father often warned him about maintaining a narrow focus on achieving tenure. Maybe he should start to listen.

He whispered, 'Can I help?'

She nodded. 'Hold Santos's paws,' she whispered back.

'What are you planning?'

She huffed out a breath. 'Just do it.'

He complied. When her hands moved to open the dog's mouth, he cautioned, 'Careful. He might bite. Let me.'

'It's okay,' she murmured. 'I've seen this done before, and he trusts me. He won't bite.'

'You can't be sure of that.'

'I am.'

Damn, she was stubborn. Alex lowered his tone. 'Nikki . . . '

She looked at him. '*Alex*. I know what I'm doing, so do what I say, okay?' Her mouth curved in a don't-patronize-me-buster smile as the chilly mountain breeze ruffled her sunshine-blonde curls and goose bumps budded on her bare arms.

'Alllll right.' She definitely had a way

155

of convincing a guy.

He held Santos's paws while she stroked the dog's head. 'There's my good boy,' she soothed in a soft voice Alex wouldn't mind hearing in the middle of the night. 'Santos is a *gooood* boy.' Gingerly, she examined the dog's mouth and tongue. 'None inside. He was lucky.'

She glanced at Alex again. 'There are pliers in the drawer by the kitchen sink. I just boiled some water for tea. Please use what's left in the kettle to sterilize the pliers and then bring them out to me. Also, fetch a paper towel to hold the quills after we pull them. Take Bernie with you and leave him in the cabin. I don't want him sniffing around for the porcupine while we're busy.'

'Gotcha.' Alex couldn't deny those baby blues. His white-knight instincts wouldn't let him.

Or so he rationalized as he grabbed a growling Bernie and jogged to the cabin.

However, as he deposited the Chihuahua indoors, common sense dictated there was more going on with him than a need to play the hero. He'd 'rescued' his sisters countless times without once feeling compelled to stare at their breasts. He couldn't dismiss his response to Nikki as part of some big-brother persona.

Minutes later, he returned with the sterilized pliers and a chunk of paper towel, the flip-flops crunching in the tall grass. Bernie hadn't been thrilled with his confinement in the cabin, although a sprinkle of kibble in the dog's food dish had mollified him . . . a bit. While the little guy possessed a perpetual mad-on for Alex, the Saint Bernard treated him like a well-chewed shoe. A few tongue-slurps and affectionate drools were commonplace.

What an idiot he'd been, allowing the ancient critter to wander off. Santos hadn't meant the porcupine any harm. The big guy was only curious.

Alex knelt beside Nikki and Santos. She reached for the pliers, but Alex held them firm. 'I'll do this.'

Her eyebrows lifted. 'Have you removed quills before, on your dad's farm?'

'My father grows potatoes. They have eyes, not snouts. And they sure don't tend to wander.'

'They just kind of vegetate then, I guess.'

He smiled. 'Just kind of.'

'Well, I watched my grandfather de-quill his black Lab back in the day. And I've assisted Dr. Green a few times at work.'

'You work?' He'd imagined her primping for a life of leisure with Royce, a visual that grew more irksome by the second.

She chuckled. 'I'm a vet's assistant.'

He stared at her. Her love for animals, her calm reaction to Santos's plight, her comments about anesthetic and canine plaque removal . . .

Bingo!

Never assume, he told his freshman history classes. Always do the research.

He should take his own advice. Nikki never failed to surprise him.

She slipped the pliers and paper towel from his grasp, her soft skin brushing his fingers. 'We've established that I'm the authority figure here, so listen up,' she said. 'And you don't have to give me that stunned look, Alex.' She prodded his thigh with the pliers. 'Not all girls raised with silver spoons in their mouths choose to live off their trust funds. My paycheck's a pittance, but I love what I do. And I try to live within my means.' Her eyes clouded. 'Until I marry Royce. Then everything changes.'

'Like what?'

'It doesn't matter.' She set aside the paper towel. 'Back to business.' She gestured to Santos. 'Most dogs accept the quills after a while, when they only have a few, like my fella. And Santos has such a gentle nature. He knows we're trying to help him.' She stroked the dog's floppy ears. 'Don't you, boy?'

Santos moaned as he woofed, his baggy eyes centered on her.

And only her.

She cooed to the dog. 'Move behind him,' she instructed Alex. 'Hold his head.'

After he'd followed her directions, she continued, 'Cover his eyes with one hand, if you can. That's it.'

She swept in with the pliers, gripped a quill, and tugged. Santos's head almost jerked out of Alex's grasp. However, the dog's reflexes couldn't match their teamwork.

Holding up the pliers, Nikki displayed a long, hollow quill. 'There, you see? He helped me pull it out.' She wiped away the dot of blood marring Santos's white fur. 'We'll allow him a minute to recover before trying another quill. If we take our time, he'll let us remove every one. Then we'll wash the wounds to prevent infection.' She deposited the quill on the paper towel.

'You're amazing,' Alex murmured. And damn it if he didn't mean it.

She blushed. 'No, I'm not.'

'Yes, you are.' She tended to her dog

like a mother would a hurt child. With love, gentle care, a sweet smile, a soft kiss, a firm touch when needed. Like Alex could imagine her behaving with her own children someday.

Children he suddenly and absurdly wished *he* could father instead of Royce.

She was beautiful. And trusting. Undeserving of the pain and heartache that most likely awaited her at the hands of her fiancé.

His chest tightened. 'I'm staying.'

She gazed at him. 'I know you are.'

'No. Now I'm really staying — until Royce comes or you tell me to get lost. I'm here for you, Nikki. I promise.'

Her smile warmed him like summer sunshine. 'I never doubted it for a second . . . sort of.'

★　★　★

'So you earned your degree in biology three years ago and then started working for this Dr. Green?' Nikki's guest reiterated before glancing up from his half-eaten baked potato. Alex's gaze zeroed in on her, and she squirmed on the picnic table in front of the cabin. His back faced the property sloping down towards the shore and dock while she enjoyed the panoramic lake and mountain views in the dwindling rays of evening sun. She'd tried offering him the better seat, but he was too polite. Too considerate. Super nice.

'It's clear you love animals, and you're definitely no dummy,' he said. 'You don't need a bachelor of science to assist someone. Why didn't you continue to vet school?'

She fiddled with the sleeve of the sweater she'd donned over her T-shirt before they'd begun barbecuing. Urgh, how to answer his question? With honesty or . . . a version of the truth?

Usually, during these getting-to-know-you situations, she trotted out the conversation she liked to think of as *My Life Before Royce, the Condensed Version*. The unabridged edition took too long to relate. Besides, describing the years of disappointing her parents depressed her.

However, Alex was different from the men and women she typically encountered in Royce's social circles. Take this morning, for instance. During Alex's sojourn to the shed with Murray, he hadn't run away from her like a screaming survivor of the zombie apocalypse — like the vast majority of Royce's buddies would have. Instead, he'd stayed and helped her de-quill Santos.

He was helping her *now*, remaining at the cabin until her fiancé arrived. She swallowed a bite of steak. 'Um, I didn't say my father realized I majored in Biology.'

Alex's head tipped. 'No kidding. What did he think you majored in?'

'Art History.'

'That's a far cry from Biology, Nik. Hey, I'm a historian. I should know.'

'Well, it couldn't be helped. I had to fool him.' She tossed a tidbit of steak to

163

Bernie sitting at attention on the lawn. A few feet away from his canine brother, Santos gnawed the bone from Alex's meal, and Rusty napped on the bench beside her. 'Father never would have allowed me to major in the sciences, much less attend vet school. At eighteen, I had no backbone. I tried discussing the issue during my first two years, but he was adamant.' Tucking in her chin, she mimicked her father's commanding tone, 'Education in and of itself is a fine thing, but a woman knows her place, Nicole. Strive to be a daughter I can be proud of, like Gillian.' She dropped the impersonation. 'The ever-perfect Gillian,' she muttered.

Alex lifted his fork. 'Are you sure your father's not in petroleum? He's a dinosaur, Nikki. No one thinks like that anymore.'

'Not in the Hart family, maybe.'

'What about your mom?'

'Mother thinks what she's told to. As long as the money's rolling in, she's happy.' As happy as a woman in a loveless marriage could manage, at any rate.

'So you're telling me if you'd been born Nicholas instead of Nicole, you'd be managing your own vet clinic by now, with your father's blessing?'

'That's about it.' She sighed. 'However, even if I'd been born a boy, I'm afraid veterinary medicine isn't my father's idea of, well, medicine.'

'But dermatology is?' Alex took another bite of his baked potato drenched in sour cream.

'Any specialty would suffice — for a boy. Gillian married an ear, nose, and throat man in Chicago, and Father was ecstatic. Ear, nose, and throat? Can you imagine looking up people's noses for a living? Yet Stewart, Gillian's husband, looks *down* his nose at the very patients who own the noses he looks into!' She waved her steak knife. Every time she thought of the snob appeal Stewart possessed in polyps for someone like her father, steam practically blasted from her ears. 'The point is, I'm a woman, Alex. In the world according to Geoffrey St. James, my place is behind my man — not in front of him, and probably not even beside him. I've fought his archaic attitude my entire life, and it's gotten me nowhere.'

'Unbelievable. My sisters wouldn't stand for that kind of stuff from my dad, Nik. Neither would my mom. She'd throw him a spade and tell him to start shoveling.'

'But everyone in your family supports each other.' They'd talked about his sisters and parents while grilling the steaks. The easy affection and closeness he'd relayed were foreign to her. 'Your folks respect and accept your choices. If they were anything like my parents, your life might have turned out very different.'

He waggled his fork, gazing at her as she rambled.

'Biology was quite simply out,' she continued. 'Unless I was sneaky about it, taking the necessary prerequisites and declaring my major on the sly. I hated lying to my parents, though. And please don't think I've developed a nasty habit of tricking people, because I haven't.' Her campus caper and this weekend marked the two occasions during which she'd attempted to pull a fast one. 'But Father's attitude backed me into a corner. He was remarkably easy to deceive. One, 'Yes, I'll major in Art History, like Gillian did,' and he was satisfied. I managed the online stuff, and it didn't occur to him to double-check.'

Her father's acceptance of her bald-faced lie hadn't been a matter of him trusting that she'd obey his old-fashioned edict, either. Her parents hadn't kept tabs on her college career, because they rarely noticed anything she did ... unless she was doing something wrong.

She cut up her remaining steak. 'He didn't blink when the credit card bills were lower than my sister's. I worked on campus to pay as much tuition as I could. He assumed I couldn't handle the class load and was getting extra help. Study groups, the student center, and so forth.'

Alex's forehead furrowed. 'When did they figure it out? They must know by now.'

'Yeah, they know.' Her voice sounded hollow, which pretty much mimicked how she felt. Her parents' disinterest in her lost dream had haunted her for far too long. 'They learned about it at my graduation, when they read the program. Dumb me, I'd hoped that if I earned great grades, my major wouldn't matter, that they might even feel proud of me. I thought Father would admire my ambition and support my goal to apply to vet school. Boy, was I wrong. He was livid. And Mother was livid because he was.' She pushed a piece of meat around on her plate. 'I was crushed. I'd so wanted to please them. But I couldn't afford vet school on my own.'

'What about student loans?'

'A possibility. However, I wanted to fix things with my parents first.'

She still did. Regardless of her motives, she'd deliberately deceived them. 'I couldn't stand being such a disappointment to them.' Too much like Gram Sorensen, as her mother constantly reminded her. Too 'high-spirited,' whatever that meant. Like she was a wild pony they needed to tame. 'So when Father said I could work at a vet clinic provided I also volunteered for charities of Mother's choosing, I jumped at the chance. I wanted to prove I could handle the obligations they considered important while also working in a field I love. Then I met Royce, through Father. He was everything my parents wanted for me — '

She wiggled on the picnic table. She sounded like she'd only started dating Royce to earn points with her parents. Yet that hadn't been the case. *No, siree.* She and Royce had felt inevitable. He'd come on to her like no other man she'd ever met. She'd fallen for him because — before they'd had sex, anyway — he'd made her feel like the only woman in the world. She hadn't been able to resist the attention he'd showered on her in the beginning. She doubted any woman as inexperienced as she had been could.

Big deal if their sex life hadn't rocked her universe when he'd proposed after eons of dating and they'd finally made love. So what if complete fulfilment seemed perpetually beyond her body's grasp?

It is better to give than to receive. Half a loaf is better than none.

Except, the tiny stabs of pleasure she experienced whenever Royce . . . dallied . . . down there before proceeding to the main event felt more like one-twentieth of the sensations her girlfriends boasted about.

Maybe if he dallied more often, she'd get the hang of this business. But he was always in a hurry to reach the main event!

'Nikki? Uh, Nik, you in there?'

She blinked. How long had she zoned out? 'Royce was everything I wanted for *myself*,' she corrected. *Damn, that doesn't sound right, either.* 'He was — is — was — *is* — ' *Phew!* ' — everything I could possibly want in a man.'

Cripes, all that obsessing about lovemaking had turned her brain to mush and her mouth to jelly. With luck, Alex would act the gentleman and let her slip of the tongue slide away.

Nope. Not happening. His gaze zoomed in on her again, the hazel irises compelling and the sharp professor's mind lurking behind them too darn perceptive.

'You sure about that?'

'Of course. Why would you think otherwise?' Maybe because she'd strayed waaayyy beyond the boundaries of *My Life Before Royce, the Condensed Version*. She'd unabridged like crazy.

No wonder Alex doubted her conviction. He was too easy to talk to, so she'd spilled her guts — an indication she wasn't sure about anything.

'Wait, forget I asked that.' She put down her fork and knife.

His gaze focused in another smidgen. 'Why?'

'Because . . . I don't want to talk about it.'

'Because Royce isn't here yet?'

Exactly.

She blew out a breath. 'Well, I can't expect him to cancel his appointments and zip here on a moment's notice, can I?' Okay, she'd thought her fiancé would do that very thing. However, his delay had prompted her to reconsider. 'Maybe he's waiting until Monday to reschedule. His patients rely on him, you know. Maybe he had car trouble, like I mentioned this morning. Maybe he's hurt and in the hospital, or lying in a ditch somewhere.'

That last scenario didn't ring true. If Royce had been in an accident, the police would have sent word to Seattle. *Someone* would have contacted her, probably Karin.

Despite the fact that Nikki hadn't brought her cell, her cousin would have taken whatever steps necessary to alert the local authorities, who then would have arrived at Lake Eden by car or horse or flying pig to inform *her*.

Besides, wouldn't Nikki sense it if Royce had suffered a tragedy? Didn't soul mates possess a weird, cosmic connection that served them in times of dire need?

Don't ask THAT, an inner voice jangled, *unless you're prepared to hear the answer*.

Stomach cramping, she rose. The breeze rustled her sweater. She scooped up Rusty. Amid the cat's mewling, she announced, 'It's getting cold, and I'm not hungry anymore. I'm going in.'

'Nikki, wait.' Alex grabbed the cutlery, their glasses and plates. He trailed her along the wood-chip path with the dogs in tow. Like a neurotic support group, they wouldn't let her out of their sight.

She booted open the cabin door. It creaked closed behind her silent entourage.

After freeing Rusty and dividing the last of her steak between the dogs, Nikki scraped the remains of her meal into the garbage, then tidied the kitchen. Alex assisted her, remaining quiet. The silence — broken only by the dogs' chomps and Rusty's meows — thickened. Alex turned to put a dried plate in the cupboard, and Nikki slid a glance his way.

Would he really not say another word unless she indicated she was ready?

Her insides softened. He truly was a good guy. Until now, she hadn't honestly believed they existed. She'd been operating under the illusion that she needed to make the best of what — or who — life placed in her path.

Whistling, he continued drying and storing dishes. As she rinsed soapsuds down the drain, she scoped him out from beneath lowered lashes. A girl couldn't act *too* inconspicuous while eyeing her fiancé's best man.

In the dim light, Alex's nutmeg-brown hair fell in thick shocks over his forehead. Wearing her grandfather's ill-fitting clothes, he should look like a hillbilly moonshiner. Instead, masculinity radiated off him, and her heart thumped.

Stress. That's all it is. She was attracted to Royce, not Alex.

But her thoughts refused to cooperate. They kept returning to Alex. Only thirty-something hours had passed since she'd grabbed him. However, the time frame seemed much longer. Not because he was a yawner to hang out with, either, but because he sparked loose a nervous tension inside her — a kaleidoscope-of-butterflies sensation that energized her as much as their kiss had this morning.

Their kiss . . . in this very kitchen.

Their act of betrayal against Royce.

Her face burned. *Enough scoping!*

Cheeks tingling, she yanked shut the faucet and scurried to the main room, the weight of Alex's gaze plastered to her back. This time, he didn't follow.

She sat at the piano bench around the corner, heart skittering. Next, she'd hyperventilate. All because of some harmless scoping.

She pressed a palm to her chest to slow her rapid breathing. Her other hand rested on the keyboard lid of the old upright piano. She smoothed the dark wood with her fingertips like she'd loved to do as a child, her grandmother sitting beside her.

Smiling, she lifted the lid and caressed the worn, yellowed keys. She hadn't played in ages. As a kid, she'd resented the lessons her parents had insisted upon, although she'd tried her hardest to please the crabby teacher. However, this piano was different from the black lacquer monstrosity dominating her mother's living room.

This piano sang from the depths of its soul — out of tune and not giving a damn.

She tested the keys and then played

from memory. A bit choppy and discordant, but there nonetheless, a part of her.

Seconds later, the music rushed back to her, flooding her veins, and her fingers danced a rhythm along the sticky keys. She let the music flow through her, spirit soaring as she delivered the last chord.

Alex's footsteps echoed on the plank floor. 'That was beautiful,' he murmured from behind her. 'What is it?'

She glanced up. 'Franz Liszt. '*Liebestraum*,' or 'Dream of Love' in English. Parts of it, anyway. I botched the middle.'

'Not to me, you didn't.'

'Ten years of lessons.' She rubbed her hands on her white jeans. 'I'm sorry about earlier, Alex. I keep going bonkers on you. First outside, then in the kitchen.'

'It's okay.' He sat beside her on the piano bench. His flannel shirtsleeve brushed her sweater-clad arm, and her heart bounced around in her chest. Most annoying.

'What's a piano doing in a summer

cabin?' His large hands settled on the old keys, and he touched a finger to the ebonies. A screech-owl-like, high C-sharp rang out.

'Gram played, and she missed it when they spent summers here. One year, Gramps surprised her with a new piano for the farmhouse. He brought this one to the cabin so she wouldn't have to go without her music, but he could never convince a piano tuner to make the same trek.'

Alex smiled. *E, F.* The out-of-key ivories tinkled. 'He loved her.'

Nikki nodded. 'Their marriage . . . you know, that's the kind of marriage I want. Love, tenderness, companionship. Not like my parents' marriage, which is about money and prestige. I want the real thing.'

'Hmm.' He picked at the keys again. *D, G, A-flat, B.* 'The real thing includes passion.'

Her palms prickled on her thighs. 'I know. But Gram and Gramps had that, too.'

'And you have it with Royce?'

No.

Omigosh, did Alex know her secret?

'You either have it or you don't, Nik. It's not a trick question.'

His thigh grazed hers on the piano bench as he shifted closer. Just close enough. His body heat seeped into her, through her. Warmth pooled. Low, then lower.

Her breath fluttered in her throat.

His head turned, and his gaze scanned her face. His eyes, brimming with promise, captured hers with a tortuous hunger that wouldn't let go.

Her lips trembled. 'Alex?' This was it. She had to kiss him. The need burned within her, drowning her with an intensity that filled all the lonely places inside her.

How could she not have known she was so lonely?

Resting her hand on his shoulder, she gripped the soft flannel of his shirt . . . the width of elastic suspender and rock-solid muscle beneath. As if he read her thoughts — as if he felt as strongly as she did — he cradled her face with his large hands, and she tilted her chin, offering her mouth.

And then he took what she offered.

Their mouths joined . . . a slow, warm mating. A heat that pulsed with want and need such as Nikki had never known or even realized existed.

Sweet saints above, Roy's kisses had *never* moved her like this. Her heart, her soul, every fiber of her being, craved and longed for Alex.

If she burst into flames at his mere kiss, how would it feel to make love with him?

But she couldn't. *They* couldn't. Because of Roy — uh, *Royce*.

A different kind of heat seared her body. The burn of betrayal, not passion.

She pulled away, pressing her fingers to her mouth, where Alex's kiss tingled. Her engagement ring glittered, taunting her.

'Alex, what must you think of me?

Omigosh, I'm sorry. I don't know why I did that.'

'Me, neither,' he murmured. 'But I know I want to do it again.'

'We can't! Alex, that wasn't an ordinary kiss. Definitely not a practice kiss. I'm engaged!'

He studied her. 'Nikki, you're being made a fool of,' he said quietly. 'Royce isn't the knight in shining armor you believe.'

'Don't say that!' She jumped off the bench. 'Roy-oyce is my fiancé, and he loves me. I'm the one being disloyal.'

'Roy-oyce?' Alex's eyebrows rose.

'Royce.' She couldn't even get his name right. Kissing Alex had scrambled her brains as well as her emotions. How could she kiss one man while professing to love another? How could she forget herself — and forget Royce, apparently — so easily?

More questions she didn't want to answer.

Ignorance is bliss. A faithful heart

never wanders . . . or wonders.

Don't borrow trouble, as Gram used to say. Count your blessings. One-twentieth of a loaf is better than none.

7

Where There's a Willie...

'Rusty? Rusty! Where are you, fella? Come out, baby. Rusty?'

Alex paused in his shaving, the razor Nikki had given him resting on his jaw. The bathroom door sat open an inch. Over the last two days, he'd mastered the technique for allowing shower steam to dissipate without arousing the dogs' curiosity enough to pester him. Shifting his gaze in the chipped mirror, he spied the reflection of Nikki's sexy rear bobbing as she searched beneath her bed for her cat. Faded jeans hugged her hips, and a scooped-neck T-shirt the cheerful blue of a robin's eggs skimmed her torso.

Grinning, he adjusted the mirror for a better look. Her rear bounced again, and his hand jerked, the blade nicking his skin. He dragged in air through his teeth. *Damn*.

He pressed a finger to the wound. That would teach him for ogling her. Saturday night, when she'd pulled away from their kiss, she'd made it clear she didn't want an encore. Alex wasn't certain she'd meant it — she'd responded to him as naturally as if they'd been together for years — but when a woman said no, he listened.

And when that woman was Nikki St. James, confused and hurt and pining for Royce, he listened triple-hard.

So hands off. *And thoughts off.* Her vulnerability might lead her to do something she'd regret, and he wouldn't take advantage of Nikki.

Not now.

Not ever.

He finished shaving. After dabbing the bleeding spot with tissue, he readjusted her grandfather's suspenders to prevent them from cutting into his shoulders. As he entered the main room, she got up.

'Alex, have you seen Rusty?' Beside her, Santos barked, and Bernie whipped in circles on Alex's bed, snapping at the dust motes floating in the mid-morning sun.

'Yeah, I've seen him.' His head ached from the memory. He'd woken to the fantasy-inspiring sounds of Nikki in the shower to discover the cat curled atop his skull like a Davy Crockett raccoon cap with claws. When he'd moved, the claws had imbedded in his hair and skin. Knowing when he was beat, he'd scanned the rafters for cobwebs until Rusty had loosened his grip. Then he'd bent his neck, and the cat had tumbled off, racing away for an unknown destination. At that point, Alex hadn't cared. 'You were in the shower. Then I walked the dogs, and, nope, I haven't seen him since.'

'You took out the dogs?' Nikki picked a thumbnail.

'I had to. Bernie was going haywire, and Santos was pawing the doors. It was either take them out or risk them whizzing on the floor.'

'Did you leave the door open?'

'The back one. But only long enough to consider returning for some, um, reading material. It was open thirty seconds, maybe a minute at most.'

Her eyes widened. 'Oh no! Alex, Rusty's disappeared. He does this whenever we're someplace new. He knows I like him to stay indoors for a few days unless I'm with him, so he runs away the first chance he gets.' She sat on the bed and yanked on tennis shoes. 'It's not your fault. I should have warned you.'

'We'll find him.' Alex sat beside her. Similar to Saturday night, their thighs barely touched, yet heat zinged him to the bone. She scooted away and diligently tied her shoes.

No spontaneous lip-locks were forthcoming this bright Monday morning, he concluded, regret eddying.

Work with it, Hart. She doesn't need the aggravation.

Her loyalties rested with Royce. He

needed to accept that or break her heart by telling her that the schlep oozed slime.

He patted her back, big-brother style. The tissue from his shaving mishap dislodged from his jaw and landed on his clean pair of gray polyester pants. *Smooth*.

'Rusty knows which side his bread is buttered on, Nik.' He maintained a reassuring tone. 'Even if we don't find him right away, he'll return when he's hungry. Don't worry about him encountering the porcupine. Santos probably scared it. I doubt it's hanging around.'

She bolted off the bed. 'It's not the porky. What if Rusty's lost? He has no teeth.'

Alex chuckled. 'Rusty has *fangs*, honey. I've seen them.' They hung over the cat's furry chin like metal spikes, one satanically longer than the other.

'Yes, he has fangs and he has tiny front teeth, but he doesn't have molars. He can catch a bird, but if he's lost and starving, the most he can hope for is to gum it to death. That's why I give him soft food. He can chew it easier than the dry stuff.'

'Okay.' One mystery — the need for the smelly, canned food — was solved, but another had arisen. 'What happened to your cat's teeth?' he asked as he pushed bare feet into the loafers she'd retrieved from the van yesterday morning along with his practically empty laptop case. 'He doesn't look old.' He trailed her through the back door, and she closed the dogs inside. When she faced him, her pale curls glistened in the sparkling sunlight, framing her delicate features.

Beautiful. However, his maxim remained: hands off.

She wasn't his, and she never would be.

'Rusty's not old,' she said. 'He's seven. He's had periodontal problems since he was two, though.' They tramped through the tall grass near the shed, searching and calling for the cat.

'Mrs. Dibble — Rusty's first owner — didn't bring him to the clinic as often as she should have. She didn't neglect him on purpose. She just didn't realize that he was developing a serious problem. None of her other Rusties were prone to gingivitis.'

Curiouser and curiouser.

'Her other Rusties?' Alex echoed. He opened the shed door and peered into the shadowy interior. Murray stared from his new home on a cluttered worktable. A spider explored the moose head's left nostril, but Rusty — of the Dibble Rusties — was nowhere in residence. 'How many cats named Rusty had she owned?'

'Five before my Rusty, all orange tabbies.' Nikki headed behind the shed, calling for the cat. Alex stayed close to her. 'When Rusty Number Five died, Mrs. Dibble's daughter decided her mother needed something different. So Dora gave Mrs. Dibble a sealpoint Siamese kitten. And Mrs. Dibble named him Rusty.'

Alex chuckled. 'I'd wondered how he'd earned his name. Why didn't Mrs. Dibble keep him?'

Nikki slid a hand through her hair, and her angel-curls bounced as she peeked into the heavy brush. 'He requires too much care for a seventy-five-year-old woman living alone. Mrs. Dibble noticed that Rusty shook his head when he ate — a sign a cat's gums are inflamed. She thought nothing of it until he took ill. Even then, she didn't understand what was making him sick. The poor fella nearly died of toxin absorption brought on by gingivitis.'

Parting the brush, she uttered squeaky bird noises. Alex joined her in the undergrowth, remaining a few feet behind so he wouldn't spook the cat.

'Rusty's back teeth were practically falling out,' she continued between bird imitations. 'Dr. Green had to pull them. He could have put the cat to sleep, but the thought upset Mrs. Dibble terribly. She felt awful that she'd allowed the problem to progress to such a point.

She couldn't afford the surgery, so I offered to pay. She was so grateful Rusty didn't have to be put down that she asked if I wanted to keep him. Of course I said yes. The chances of a cranky, semi-toothless cat getting chosen at an animal shelter are tragically slim.'

'She didn't plan on taking him home?'

'No. Alex, it was so sad. She worried about any upcoming bills. If I didn't want him, she hoped a loving family would take pity on him and adopt him. The truth was, if a shelter was Rusty's next stop, he was likely headed for an eternal nap. After the discomfort he'd suffered, I couldn't let that happen.'

'That's quite a story.' Didn't Nikki realize how generous, caring, and warm-hearted she was? Did *Royce* have any clue what a gem he'd found in this woman? 'You adopted Rusty to set Mrs. Dibble's mind at ease.' Completely Nikki.

She nodded. 'I had Bernie already, and you know he was a rescue dog, so what was one more pet? Santos strayed into my life a few months ago, and our little family grew to four, plus my roommates.'

Interesting that she didn't include Royce as part of her expanding 'family.'

Envisioning her future husband — a guy Alex considered a pal less and less, given the hell the creep kept putting Nikki through — allowing her animals into his pristine, high-rise apartment proved an even greater challenge.

Would Royce's condo board even allow three pets, one a massive Saint Bernard? Those fancy developments usually boasted weight and size restrictions, including rules about the common areas where a dog could and could not put down its paws.

Imagine carrying Santos to the elevators just to take the old fellow for a walk. Had Royce promised Nikki they would move? And she'd believed him?

'Rusty's a lucky cat,' he murmured glumly. 'Lucky Rusty Number Six.'

She smiled, and the dark cloud hovering over him whisked away. 'Isn't that lucky number seven?' she asked.

This from the woman who mangled clichés on an hourly basis? 'Well, he's seven years old, so he's Lucky Seven, too. Add them together, and he's Lucky Thirteen.'

She chuckled. 'Thank you, Alex.' A bee buzzed, and she waved it away from her curly hair.

'For what?' God, he wanted to touch her.

'For making me feel better. That's what you're trying to do with all your questions, so don't pretend it's not.'

'All right, I won't.' In the serenity of the overgrown, light-dappled brush, while a cacophony of insect noises and flirty birdsong thrummed amidst the fragrant wildflowers and towering evergreens, he couldn't pretend his way out of a torn gunnysack.

However, that didn't mean he'd decided to act on his growing feelings for Nikki. He might keep the truth from her, but he could finally admit it to himself.

He was dangerously close to falling in love with his sexy wood nymph — Royce Carmichael's hold on her be damned.

★ ★ ★

'Don't get excited, Nik, but I think we've found your cat. It looks like he's in trouble.'

Nikki whipped her head around. She and Alex stood behind the unoccupied cabin neighboring her grandfather's and had already scoured both properties front and back. Now, he pointed another cabin away. She spied Rusty, all right — in arched-back, bristle-tailed splendor. An old man raced from the small structure with a shovel cleaving the air. In the doorway, an elderly woman's hand shot up.

'Willie, no!' the woman called.

'It's getting away!' the man shouted back. His shovel thumped the ground, narrowly missing Rusty. 'Keep him close, tiger! That's it! We'll get him yet! Damn harbinger of evil!'

'Alex, quick!' Heart pounding, Nikki ran toward the man. 'He'll kill him!'

Alex raced past her. 'Leave that cat alone!'

The shovel thumped again. 'Crud! Missed!'

Alex dashed into the yard ahead of her. The old guy's head popped up, his mouth gaping as Alex grabbed the shovel.

'Damn it, lad! Watcha doing?'

Nikki swept in, grabbing Rusty. Heedless of the cat's flailing paws, she clutched his trembling body to her chest. 'Rusty, Rusty, are you okay?'

The cat yowled.

He's okay. Thank God. A complaining Rusty was a naturally occurring phenomenon. Mewling whimpers would have indicated that the old man had hurt him.

'Give me the shovel, boy,' Rusty's assailant demanded.

'Not on your life.' Alex gripped the handle with both hands. The old guy snatched the brittle wood, but his thin fingers waged an ineffectual battle against Alex's strong and sturdy grasp.

'Damn, boy, it's about to climb up my leg!' The old fellow shook a bare foot. 'Violet!' he called to the woman hurrying from the doorway. 'Lucifer's grandson is waging another attack! Don't you fret! I'll get him!'

He swooshed a surprisingly limber hand to the ground. Straightening, he shook his quarry — not Rusty, but a harmless little garter snake.

The man's eyes narrowed to gleeful slits. 'I'll squeeze the life from its long, skinny lungs!'

Nikki gasped. 'Don't you dare!' Rusty squirmed in her arms, paw swiping toward the snake. 'That goes for you, too.' She swatted the cat's skull. The old man posed no danger to her pet. While she'd been searching the bushes with her heart lodged in her throat, Rusty had been playing African Safari.

Alex threw down the shovel and stepped toward the old guy. 'You heard her. Drop the snake.'

'I! Will! Not!' The fellow waved the traumatized garter like a banner. His unbuttoned shirt revealed a chest flecked with white hair. The scraggly patch on his head stood up, lending him the appearance of a scruffy albino rooster. 'I am protecting my woman.' His chin whiskers jutted.

The woman in question — an eighty-ish vision in a lavender shift, fuzzy purple slippers, and a lilac tint brightening her loose white hair — neared them. Calmly, she placed a hand on his arm. 'Willie, I don't need protecting. Honestly, sugar, a little nooky and you start making like a caveman.'

'I am a man reborn,' Willie asserted. 'Vigor flows through my veins, woman. Through every single one of them, if you get my drift.' Winking at her, he chortled.

Violet clucked her tongue. 'I got your

drift not twenty minutes ago. We've two weeks, Will. We can pace ourselves. There's no need to run around half-cocked.'

'*Half?*' Willie's shoulders thrust back. He waved the snake again. 'Scoot back to bed, Vi. I'll show you 'half.' But first I'm gonna skin me a rattler.'

Nikki looked at Alex. *We have to do something*, she pleaded with her eyes.

As if in understanding, he raised a hand. She translated the gesture: *Let's give it a second.*

A breath seeping out of her, she nodded.

'For goodness sake, Will,' Violet murmured. 'It's a garter snake. If we'd closed the door, it wouldn't have entered the cabin.' She touched his arm.

Willie harrumphed. 'The fresh air invigorates me, as you well know.'

'That's not all that invigorates you, dear. Please, Will, put down the snake and then maybe I won't have to ask this nice young man — ' she smiled at Alex

' — to hit *you* with the shovel.' Her manner remained tender, loving, and oh-so-wifely reasonable.

Willie's gaze darted between his spouse and the shovel. A moment later, he lowered his arm. 'Damn, Vi, you're ruining my fun.' The snake dangled from his hand.

'I'll make up for it, sugar.'

His blue eyes brightened. 'Hot damn!' He tossed the snake over his shoulder, and it plopped onto the ground.

Nikki's heart squeezed. The poor creature!

'Wait,' she appealed to the geriatric couple, while Rusty meowed and squirmed in her embrace.

She passed the cat to Alex. Kneeling where the snake had landed in the dewy grass, she picked it up with gentle fingers. Standing, she gripped the snake's head behind its jaw, like her grandfather had taught her. A pungent odor rose from the little snake, indicating its fear. Nikki examined it for damage.

Alex walked over and studied the garter, too, but she signaled him to step back before Rusty catapulted from his hold and stormed another offensive.

Again, he comprehended her meaning. Nodding, he moved away, and her heart lightened. His willingness to follow her lead was something she hadn't experienced a lot in her personal life. It was like he actually had confidence in her. Royce would have scoffed at her attempt to help a common garter snake.

She traveled her gaze over the helpless creature. A scrape marked the dark green scales resting cool against her palm.

Frowning, she looked up. 'Mr. Gotobed, you didn't hit this poor guy, did you?'

The old fellow peered at her. 'You know me, child?'

Nikki nodded. Now that the commotion had subsided, she recognized Willie and his wife as long-time summer residents of Lake Eden, although she couldn't recall them using their cabin this early in the season. She and her sister had often visited Violet with Gram while Willie and Gramps went fishing. Willie had always been excitable, but never cruel. Certainly, Nikki hadn't ever witnessed him trying to hack up a harmless garter snake.

'I'm Nikki St. James,' she informed him. 'Hans Sorensen was my grandfather. My, uh, friend and I are spending a few days at the cabin.'

Willie's gaze narrowed further. 'I don't remember a Nikki.'

Violet smiled. 'But I bet you remember a little Nicole!'

Willie nodded. 'You're Nicole?' A wide grin split his face.

'Yes, although I go by Nikki now.' Outside her immediate family, at any rate. Despite her requests, her parents and Gillian still called her Nicole. They probably always would. Habits formed during childhood were tough to break.

Or so she told herself.

'Mr. Gotobed, the snake,' she repeated. 'There's a mark near its tail that concerns me. Did you hit it?'

'Nope.' His chest puffed. 'But I was determined to.'

'You were not,' Violet said softly. 'You were showing off, nothing more. The poor thing must have been hurt before it came into the cabin.' She looked at Nikki. 'I don't know what's gotten into my Willie . . . ' Her lips pursed. 'Well, I suppose I do.'

'Darn tooting, you do!' The morning breeze riffled his sparse white hair.

Violet ignored him. 'However, I didn't expect this reaction to the medication. I wonder if it's normal.'

'Medication, heck!' Willie whipped a tiny green pill out of his shirt pocket faster than an infomercial spokesperson. 'It's Rise-Amazing-All!'

'*Rise-All*,' Violet amended.

'*Praise* all!' Chortling, Willie turned to Alex. 'It's a proper miracle of modern science, young fellow. Fixes impertinence and promotes psychological well-being! They don't promise you the psyche thing, but I tell ya, I got it! And better than ever, eh, Vi?' He hooted.

Violet's hand fluttered to her throat. 'I can't complain. Except, dear? The word is impotence.'

'Not anymore!'

Nikki blushed. She couldn't even look at Alex, although his chuckle reached her ears. First, he confronted her about her lack of passion with Royce, and now these frisky octogenarians were staging their mating dance in public.

What secret did the Gotobeds share that she and Royce lacked? The Rise-All accounted for Willie's amorous behavior to a point. However, Willie and Violet had always been affectionate with each other. If the old fellow had endured some difficulty in the bedroom, Nikki had never witnessed evidence that the problem had debilitated their marriage.

Like her grandparents had, the Gotobeds delighted in a love that was strong and true. A love that could slay dragons and pulverize slabs of granite into rubble.

Was that kind of love lost to Nikki's generation?

She risked a glance at Alex. He cradled Rusty in his arms, his brown hair mussed by their search. Her mutinous heart pit-a-patted. *My knight in plaid flannel.*

A smiled tugged her mouth. In that moment, she scarcely noticed the snake or the randy Gotobeds. The sky, trees, lake — all faded away.

All she saw was Alex.

His gaze linked with hers, and the ground shifted beneath her feet. Her bones melted as surely as if they were molded from jelly.

Panic led a parade out of her heart. *Cupid, help me.*

She couldn't name what she was feeling, or maybe she didn't dare to. She only knew that succumbing to this soul-deep yearning would prove her engagement — and perhaps her entire life — a lie.

★ ★ ★

Seated at the cabin table, Alex glanced through the printed research notes he'd retrieved from his computer case after lunch. Trying not to be obvious about it, he kept one eye on Nikki. Sitting on the chair to his left with her legs crossed, she carefully handled the small garter snake they'd rescued from Willie Gotobed four hours earlier. A sudden downpour had sequestered them in the cabin with her thankfully napping pets, but not before she'd recruited Alex's help digging earthworms for the snake's dinner.

They'd cleaned the worms and placed them in a jar lid, which Nikki had set into a terrarium she'd located in the shed. A mixture of washed sand, potting soil, and tiny pieces of bark layered the bottom of the glass tank.

With a couple of flat rocks for sunning and a shallow bowl of water for bathing, the vivarium, as Nikki called it, featured the finest in garter snake style and comfort.

Under her direction, Alex had placed the mesh-roofed unit on a heating pad on a decorative wall shelf — beyond Rusty's reach. However, Nikki, expressing concern for the traumatized snake's welfare, continued bringing the reptile out of the enclosure for checkups.

Her compassion for the creature fascinated Alex. He'd never encountered a less squeamish woman. Granted, not many kooky animal lovers frequented PU's stodgy history department, where he spent most of his time, and lately he'd been so focused on achieving tenure that it hadn't dawned on him to date a non-colleague. However, never in his dreary existence had he imagined meeting a woman as loving, down to earth, and full of life as Nikki St. James.

He allowed his gaze to slide over her slim body, and his pulse kicked.

Battling his attraction to her grew more difficult with each passing minute. Thinking of her as Royce Carmichael's fiancée no longer helped, just made him want to beat the hell out of the jerk. Finally, he'd attempted envisioning her as the kid sister of a steroid-ridden Goliath who rode his Harley over intellectuals for sport and drank gasoline in triumph. However, even that rather imaginative effort had proven useless.

He returned his gaze to his notes.

'Alex?' she asked a moment later. 'What should we name her?'

'Huh?' He feigned absorption in his research.

'The snake.' She nudged his arm. 'We rescued her. Therefore, she needs a name. Any ideas?'

He looked at her again — in the eyes this time. The garter, apparently no longer traumatized, slipped between her fingers.

'That depends.' He set down his papers. 'How do you know it's a she?'

'I don't. But Rusty, Bernie, and Santos are all boys, so it stands to reason that the snake's a girl. That way, I'm not as outnumbered.'

Alex grinned. It stood to *her* refreshingly quirky brand of reasoning, maybe. But he wasn't about to point out her lack of logic. All day, between periods of caring for the snake, she'd practically glued her eyeballs to her watch, monitoring the time. Royce's continued absence clearly bothered her. Occupying herself with the garter snake provided a necessary diversion.

'Sounds good to me,' he said. 'She's a girl.'

'Then she needs a girl's name.' Nikki caressed her reptilian ward. The cold-blooded creature was enjoying more action than *he* had these last few months. 'Would you like to do the honors?'

'Not a chance. You're much more creative. If it were up to me, I'd call her Snake.'

She knocked his leg with her foot.

'Alex, that's boring.'

Yup, that was him. Boring. Dull. Ho-hum as week-old bran.

He hadn't always been so beige. At one time, he'd happily indulged in interests outside of PU — squash, boxing, restoring his vintage car to collector status, trips to Idaho to visit his family. Even his early academic career had excited him more than his current path in life.

As a teaching assistant, he'd thrived on interaction with his students. He'd enjoyed debating points of history, had experienced intense satisfaction and a strong measure of pride when a young mind grappling with a difficult concept broke through and produced an A paper.

When had he grown so disconnected and out of touch? The research notes for his submission to a top history journal read dry, dry, dry. The resulting article would no doubt read every bit as uninspiring even while publishing the piece would bring him another step closer to realizing his full potential by achieving tenure.

Yawn. Snore. Ho-hum.

'That's why you should name the snake,' he said. 'My muse hasn't just deserted me, she never set up camp to begin with.'

Nikki's nose scrunched. 'That's bull.'

'But true.'

'I don't believe it.'

Leaning closer, she thrust the snake beneath his nose. Her breasts plumped beneath her top, the scooped neckline exposing her slight cleavage.

'Think, Alex.' Her melodic voice sounded airy. 'What does she remind you of?'

Sin. Temptation. Apples. Fornication.

Inhaling, he lifted his gaze from her top. The garter snake slithered in her hands. Its bullet head turned and the slit of a mouth popped open.

'Uh, Lucifer's grandson?'

Nikki laughed. 'Perfect! That's what Willie called her! At first, I thought he was talking about Rusty, but — ' her gaze drifted over the snake ' — she's a girl, we've already established that, so she's Lucifer's grand*daughter*. Lucy for short.'

'Sheer genius.'

For a second, they grinned idiotically at each other.

Crash! Boom!

'Woof!' Santos's deep bark echoed in the confined space.

Nikki jumped up, the snake bouncing in her grasp as they turned toward the noise. Santos had awoken from his nap among the storage boxes and now stretched while his big tail repeatedly thumped a collapsed tower. The dog sniffed the spilled contents.

'Duty calls, Luce,' Nikki said to the snake. 'What have you found, boy?' she directed toward Santos.

Holding Lucy, she climbed onto her chair and stretched to reach the wall shelf that housed the vivarium. Alex got up and placed a hand on her hip — to steady her, no other reason. Just being a gentleman.

He snorted.

'What?' Nikki glanced down.

'Nothing.' He really, really wanted to move his hand. Mold it to her perky rear or caress her waist. Lick her belly-button ring, eat her up.

He did none of those things. Palm on fire, he maintained a semblance of noble intention while she returned Lucy to the vivarium. Face composed, he grasped her hand and steadied her as she climbed back down.

Earlier, the mosquito-dog otherwise known as Bernie had staked out his snoozing territory on Alex's bed. Now the Chihuahua bounded off, joining Alex and Nikki as they crossed the room to examine Santos's clutter. Even Rusty emerged from his vampire cave beneath Nikki's bed, meowing drowsily.

'Oh!' A bright smile lighting her features, Nikki knelt near Santos. She smoothed her hands over the slim hardcover books strewn on the blue-painted wood floor.

'What are they?' Crouching between

her and the dog, Alex selected a volume. With its worn, dusty cover and narrow spine, it resembled an ancient office record book. His historian's antennae tingled.

'My grandfather's collection of farming journals.' Wonder brimmed Nikki's voice. 'I thought my mother threw them away.'

Alex flipped over the thin volume in his hand. 'Why would she do that?'

'Who knows? Lack of interest? Farming bores her.' She picked up a journal and skimmed her fingers over the dark cover. 'I thought she chucked them out when she packed up the Poulsbo place. I didn't even know they were here.'

'Maybe she stored them for safekeeping.' The drafty lake cabin would wreak havoc on the old paper, but the grieving process often took precedence over historical preservation. And rightly so. Losing a parent must be rough.

'Hmm . . . nah,' Nikki murmured. 'More likely Gramps brought them.

Gram passed away three years before he did, but he spent his summers at Lake Eden until he died . . . two springs ago.'

'I'm sorry.'

'Thanks. And it's okay. He was eighty-nine.'

Alex nodded. 'So . . . Lake Eden. That's where we are?'

'Olympic Peninsula, off 101,' she confirmed. She eyed him. 'You won't try leaving again now that you know our location, will you?'

And cut short his time with her? 'No way.'

She graced him with another smile. 'I didn't think so. You had your chance when we ran into the Gotobeds. If you'd wanted to leave, you would have said something to them.'

The thought hadn't occurred. Man, he'd tumbled deep into the rabbit hole.

'You question my sincerity?' he teased. 'Nikki, I'm crushed.'

'No doubts. I trust you, Alex.' A light blush dusted her cheeks. Gaze flitting away, she traced the chafed corners of the dark-covered record book with her fingertips. 'Maybe Gramps brought the journals here because they helped him feel closer to Gram.' She caressed the volume. 'Most of these journals are from her side of the family. Her great-uncle began farming in 1912, and then her dad joined him. However, some of the diaries might originate from outside the family. Gramps once showed me a farm record from 1895, written in Norwegian. He'd find a journal in some country antique shop and buy it. He adored history, Alex.' She glanced up. 'Like you.'

Her smile widened until it reached her sparkling blue eyes. A current arced, electrifying the inches between them.

Alex's blood pumped. *Hell*. Royce Carmichael was nuts. How could the moron not see what was so plain to Alex? Nikki offered the idiot a lifetime of soft smiles and crazy happiness. Trust, constancy, a deep, abiding love.

The chance to build something real together.

What Alex wouldn't give to have her look at *him* the way she was looking at him right now — the way she probably always looked at Royce — every day for the rest of *his* life.

What he wouldn't give to be in Royce Carmichael's position.

Rusty slipped out from between two boxes. The cat padded across the strewn journals and rubbed his neck against the leg of Nikki's jeans. Rusty's spine curved, seeking her touch. No, more likely craving it.

Alex empathized.

You and me both, pal.

He petted the cat. *You and me both.*

8

The Jig's Up

Come Tuesday evening, Nikki had reached the sobering conclusion that Operation Fool-A-Fiancé was falling apart at the seams. That was, if it had ever *had* seams.

For one thing, the fiancé in question had yet to show. For another, she doubted he ever would, for whatever reason.

Worse, she didn't feel anywhere near as devastated by Royce's continued absence as she suspected a woman deeply in love and desperate to have her fiancé prove his love in return *should* feel.

She should feel frantic or frenzied or at least hopping mad — but she wasn't. Instead, she felt vaguely disgruntled and . . . oddly relieved. Because the longer it took Royce to arrive, the more time she had with Alex.

She squirmed on the battered sofa. For the last half-hour, she'd lounged against a cushion with her yoga pants wrinkled at her bent knees. Rusty purred on her lap while she pretended to read one of her grandmother's old medical romances discovered in a box of worn magazines and paperbacks.

Not far away, Alex sat in his usual chair at the table, engrossed in Gramps's collection of farming journals. Both Santos and Bernie snoozed as close to the poor guy's chair as possible without squashing his toes. Alex's feet sported the same type of thick wool socks currently toasting Nikki's tootsies. She'd found him a clean work shirt — blue, this time — and faded tan pants to wear. The pants, although hemmed as short as the brown ones and the gray polyesters, hailed from her grandfather's less-rotund years. In place of suspenders, Alex had cinched the baggy trousers with his belt.

As for underneath the shabby slacks . . . well . . . Alex's recently washed boxers hung drying in the bathroom for the third time since they'd arrived. Unless he stored a reserve pair in his computer case, which she would have noticed by this point, it appeared the man she'd written off as a stick-in-the-mud history professor was . . . *ahem* . . . letting things fall where they may.

Her tummy warmed, and she bit her lip.

She did not appreciate these involuntary physical responses! She'd indulged in far too many fantasies about Alex and his damn things lately. Thirty hours of pouring rain would render a desert dweller delusional, but Nikki had been born and bred in damp Seattle. Normally, she could handle a little torrential downpour. However, the coziness of the rain pattering the cabin roof these last two nights had conspired against her. As had the velvet darkness blanketing the windows. The cabin cocooned them from the elements, but exposed her to Alex's sexy earthiness.

His magic touch with her animals had lowered her defenses to a dangerous level. Santos had taken a shine to the man almost immediately. However, now Rusty and even Bernie — the lovable traitors — were developing soft spots for him.

Rusty had sheathed his claws ever since Alex had rescued the cat from Willie Gotobed's shovel. Then, last night, after Alex had fallen asleep with his newfound Siamese buddy curled beside him, Bernie had vaulted onto the bed, observed the snoozing duo, and flopped at Alex's feet.

Oh, how Nikki's heart had melted. And the fickle organ didn't seem in any hurry to re-solidify as she and Alex approached their fifth night together.

Sweet saints above, she didn't have a clue how to fight the effect the man had on her.

Did she *want* to?

Her jaw stiffened. More subversive thoughts! Unappreciated!

This morning, while Alex had showered, she'd whipped through a dozen relationship quizzes in the stack of tattered magazines she must have left here at some time or another. The attempt to rationalize or downplay her emotions had resulted in absurdly skewed quiz scores: a cock-eyed mixture of lust, love, and camaraderie for Alex, and a confusing blur of loyalty and a blah fondness for Royce.

What did it all mean?

She glared at Alex. *It's his fault.*

A moment later, the flannel-plaided professor reached for his steaming mug of coffee, and her pulse skipped.

His fault!

Gritting her teeth, she resumed reading her novel. She skimmed two pages of doctor-nurse interaction before her gaze lifted again — of its own damn accord, like in the book.

Alex had set down the mug and was flipping a journal page. He read something that inspired a chuckle, and his broad shoulders bunched beneath the work shirt. Nikki's breathing quickened.

That ugly flannel shirt must feel incredibly soft and warm beneath a woman's fingers. If she got up and went to him, placed her hands on his sides and curved them around to his chest, would he turn, look up, and welcome her? Would he gather her into his arms and then . . . *oh yes* . . . would he ravish her?

Or maybe *she* would ravish him . . .

Pleasurable goose bumps pebbled her legs and arms. *Wow.* Her whole body was coming alive for him. And only for him.

For Alex.

She shook her head. *Not again!* Her hormones were working overtime. She must be ovulating.

The only remedy was for Royce to barge in *right now* and save her from her womanly ruin.

Surely, if she saw her fiancé soon — if

she touched him, kissed him, held *him* — her attraction to Alex Hart would disappear. Then she could forget all this holed-up-in-a-cabin lust nonsense and return to the society life her parents had mapped out for her.

Correction, the life she'd *chosen*. No one had forced her to say yes to Royce. Her parents' expectations had exuded a definite pressure, but she'd decided to marry Royce on her own.

A weird sensation wiggled up her spine. Did she still want to marry him?

Well, of course she did.

Um . . . didn't she?

★　★　★

The next morning, Alex whistled as he tinkered beneath the raised van hood, replacing the distributor cap and inspecting the damage Nikki had inflicted on the old vehicle. Meanwhile, she'd remained indoors to care for Lucy. Now that the rain had stopped, she wanted the battered van running so she could putter to the nearest town and phone her cousin, Karin — a.k.a. Mugger Number Two. Supposedly, Karin could provide insight into whatever had delayed Royce.

Alex wiped a greasy palm on his pants. What if Karin's information hurt Nikki? He couldn't imagine Royce possessed a plausible excuse for his absence. Even if the schlep no longer wanted his fiancée, wouldn't male pride spur him to travel to Lake Eden and beat up Alex regardless?

Try to beat on him, at any rate. Alex would clobber the son of a gun. *Just give me a reason.*

The phone call to Karin should reveal that reason. It had better. The speculation chewed his guts. Nikki must be climbing the walls.

'When's the weddin'?' Willie Gotobed's rough voice shot through him, and Alex's skull whacked the open hood. He hadn't suffered so many attacks on his noggin in his life.

Rubbing his aching scalp, he moved

out from beneath the hood. 'Willie, don't sneak up on me.'

'I weren't sneaking. You were day-dreaming.'

'I was concentrating.' Neither he nor Nikki had seen Willie or Violet in the two days since Nikki had rescued Lucy from the old guy's shovel. Come to think of it, they hadn't discussed how to handle the elderly couple's potential questions about their joint presence at the cabin, either. 'What did you say again?'

'The weddin',' Willie repeated, squinting against the mid-morning sun. Santos stood panting behind him. Several feet away, Bernie frolicked with a butterfly, his Rambo complex in apparent remission. 'She's wearing an engagement ring. Don't tell me that don't mean something.'

Alex cleared his throat. 'The wedding date isn't set yet.'

'Damn kids these days! Living in sin, is she?'

'No, sir.' Alex closed the van hood.

'Nikki and I don't live together, and the cabin has two beds. Nothing shady is going on.'

Willie cackled. 'I hope not. You're not the fee-an-say!'

'I'm not?' There went one cover story.

'Nope.' Willie grinned broadly. 'I can tell.'

What a load. 'How?'

The old man smacked his lips. 'Well, now, you look at her like you *want* her to be yours, but you don't touch her like she *is* yours. No hand-holding or pecks on the cheek that we could see the other day, anyhow. What kind of fee-an-say does that make you? A fee-an-say she calls 'friend'?' He snorted, pulling his chin. 'Me and Vi guessed right off that somethin' fishy was going on. *You're* not the fee-an-say, but some other fellow is. Whether Nikki is living with the other fellow or not makes no never mind. She's here with you, and that ain't right.'

Five days ago, Alex would have

agreed with him. Hell, three days ago, he would have. But a lot had changed between then and now. Nikki trusted him, and he respected and admired her. She needed protecting from Royce. Until the mystery of the man's absence was solved, Alex was staying put.

Stepping to the driver's door, he lifted a hand. 'Mr. Gotobed — '

The old guy harrumphed. 'Vi's inside with her now, trying to wrestle the truth from the gal. Nikki's grandpa was a good friend of ours. We're determined to look out for her. Can't make whoopee all day, you know.' He cackled.

Oh brother. 'Mr. Gotobed, I realize your intentions are honorable, but — '

'What?' Willie's gaze narrowed. 'He's done her wrong, hasn't he? And you're her go-to guy, that it? We've had two days to think on this, boy, so don't be avoiding me now.'

Alex proceeded to do exactly that. He climbed behind the wheel of the van, one leg dangling out the open door. No surprise, Willie followed, Santos lumbering behind him. Bernie remained in butterfly-chasing mode.

Alex turned the key in the ignition, and the engine hacked to life. He tilted his head. 'Connection's there, but I should time it.'

Willie hitched up his pants. 'I got a timing light.'

'Nikki's grandfather probably stored one in the shed. That place is packed.'

'Well, you don't want to find yourself stranded when no one else is around. My shed's damn full herself, as she should be.' The old man's whiskered jaw shifted back and forth. 'Tell you what, lad. I'll assist you, but you gotta help me first. Violet's going crazy worrying about that little gal in there. Says she'll hide my Rise-All if I can't get you to talk. Now, cuddling is fine for old Willie, don't get me wrong, but a man starts hankering for something more after a spell. After sixty-five years of matrimony, I still want my woman. I just need the

Rise-All to do something about it.'

Alex chuckled. The randy geezer was persistent . . . and perceptive. Willie had zeroed in on Alex's feelings for Nikki like an arrow hitting its mark.

That didn't change matters, though. The story wasn't his to tell.

If the Gotobeds had arrived Friday night, he would have spilled Nikki's scheme in an instant. However, these past few days at the cabin had smacked him in the teeth with the knowledge that he'd been living his life like a gerbil on a treadmill. Yeah, he hopped off for a day or two every several months, but his rigid mindset regarding tenure always sent him racing back to PU before he could realize he'd been working too hard and too damn long for the wrong things.

He shook his head. 'Sorry, it's not my place to say anything.' He killed the engine.

'It is if you care for her. And I know you do.'

Cared for her? Hell, he loved her.

The truth sank into his bones. He loved the woman after five short nights and six incredible days. He probably would have fallen for her the first time he'd laid eyes on her — if that meeting had occurred before her engagement party.

He loved her, although he knew he shouldn't. He loved her even though it was wrong. He didn't want to see her hurt or made to feel ridiculous. According to what she'd revealed about her childhood, she'd felt deficient or somehow lacking her entire life. Her grandparents and cousin were the only close relatives who hadn't tried to change her.

As a testament to her strength of character, she'd wound up nothing like her snobby parents and sister. The personal tidbits Alex had gleaned from Hans Sorensen's farming journals seemed to indicate that Nikki resembled her deceased grandmother from her angel-kissed looks to her bubbly personality.

The cabin door creaked open, sparing him more Rise-All discussion.

Nikki and Violet emerged.

Alex climbed out of the van. As Nikki's gaze met his, she smiled, and the throbbing in his head eased. She'd acted anxious as a spooked cat all morning, startling whenever he'd neared her. Talking with Violet must have calmed her. But what had she told the old lady?

'Damn,' Willie muttered with a sideways glance. 'She better not hide my Rise-All after this.'

'Oh, I don't know, Willie. That might be fun. A sharp fellow like you should have no trouble finding it. Then you could surprise her.' Alex winked.

'Hah! You got a point there, son. Not sure I wanna trick my woman, though.'

'Hey, can you help it if she interrupted us before you could break me?'

'I like the way you think, boy!'

'The way he thinks about what, Will?' Violet asked as the women approached. She wore her purple-tinged hair in a bun today and shoes instead of slippers with her pink dress. Near her, Nikki bent to pet Santos.

'The way he thinks about . . . timing lights.' Willie elbowed Alex. 'He's working on the engine.'

'The van's nearly ready,' Alex informed Nikki. Her gaze lifted from her dog, and color tipped her cheeks.

A trace of her earlier nervousness had returned, burnished with a deeper emotion she struggled to suppress. Alex sensed the battle in the crystal-blue depths of her eyes and the barely noticeable hitch of breath in her throat.

Had she guessed how he felt about her and now wrestled with the unexpected complication?

'Turns out I don't need the van this morning after all,' she said, straightening and wiping her hands. 'But thanks for getting it running again. I appreciate it, considering I'm responsible for wrecking it in the first place.'

'You don't need the van?' Alex asked. 'What about that phone call you needed to make?'

Violet waved a hand. 'She doesn't have to go to town to make a call, dear. We have a cell phone in our cabin. Our sons insisted we bring one.'

'Yup.' Willie nodded. 'Tried telling the lads that second-honeymooners have no use for Mr. Alexander Graham Bell, but would they listen?' He grinned. 'It's like I said, you don't wanna find yourself stranded when no one else is around.' His gaze honed in on Alex. 'I'm surprised you didn't think of that yourself, young fellow.'

Nikki cringed. 'Alex left his phone in Seattle.'

'I really can't remember where,' Alex said.

'Eh?'

'Now, Will, don't pry,' Violet admonished her husband. 'Nikki needs to use our phone. That's all you have to know.' She slipped her arm through Nikki's. 'Come along, dear. The sooner you call, the better.'

'I'll go, too.' Alex closed the van door.

If Nikki heard bad news, he wanted to be there for her.

'No,' she said softly, not meeting his gaze. 'I need to do this on my own.'

Every instinct he possessed screamed that she needed his support. But he had to respect her choices — for her life and in this moment.

Stomach roiling, he nodded.

Instructing the dogs to remain behind, Nikki left with Violet.

'There *is* somethin' fishy happening.' Willie rested his hand on Alex's shoulder. 'Best let her go, son. There's no stopping them when their minds are set.' His gaze drifted to his departing wife. 'You don't think she'll still hide my Rise-All after this, do you?'

* * *

'Bidwell and Lancelot, Chartered Accountants. Good morning, this is Karin Russell. May I help you?'

'Karin,' Nikki murmured into the Gotobeds' cell phone in the privacy of their cabin bedroom. The signal sputtered but would have to do. Her attraction to Alex was rapidly growing out of hand. She needed relief before she jumped him again. Only this time she didn't have kidnapping in mind. She'd rip off his clothes and devour the man — unless she connected with Royce pretty damn soon. However, diverging from the backup plan and calling her fiancé without first checking in with Karin didn't sound smart. After the emotional upheaval of the last several days, a modicum of sanity was in order.

'Nikki?' Worry shadowed Karin's voice. 'Is that you?'

The signal crackled in Nikki's ear. 'Yes. Can you talk?'

'Thank God, it is you! I didn't know how to reach you other than driving up there. I asked for a day off, but Mr. Bidwell said he couldn't spare me after I had to leave early last week.' To help Nikki with her ridiculous plan. 'A bookkeeper fell ill, and I'm covering for her. The earliest I could have managed is Friday night. I'm sorry.'

'Don't be.' Karin hadn't worked for the accounting office long, and if she wanted to move beyond the reception desk she needed to grab opportunities as they arose. 'That's excellent news about the bookkeeping, and I should have brought my cell.' Nikki hadn't wanted to risk Alex finding her phone and using it to contact help. But hindsight was better than foresight — or something. She'd created this mess. Now she had to fix it.

She sat on a chair beside the bed. A floral housecoat draped one pillow, and Willie's prescription bottle of Rise-All tablets perched on the pine night table. Beyond the floor-length curtain that served as a bedroom door, Violet's light footfalls echoed in the kitchen area.

The woman empathized with Nikki's predicament, and that felt good. Back at her cabin, when Nikki had poured out the truth of her situation, Violet hadn't judged her. The old lady had sat down and listened, Nikki's hand clasped in hers.

In ten minutes, Nikki had enjoyed more understanding from her new friend than she had from either of her parents over the last few years.

Yet surely *she* bore some responsibility for the pathetic state of her family relationships.

She'd think more about that later.

'Royce isn't here,' she told Karin. 'He never showed. What happened?' Even if he'd planned to dump her, wouldn't he have wanted to pile on the guilt by doing it in person?

'I, um, was hoping you would have come home by now,' Karin's voice carried over the cell.

'I couldn't. I'm still waiting for Royce. Did he find the note? Did he call you? Did *you* call him? What did he say?'

A pause elapsed. 'Well, no, I didn't *call* him. I waited until Sunday and then I went over there, like you asked.'

Her cousin's reluctance to give a

straight answer clanged like a fire alarm. Getting up, Nikki paced the tiny bedroom. How Royce responded to her needs before they got married would determine his behavior once they were husband and wife — if they made it to the altar. After so much freaking hassle over setting a simple wedding date, she harbored major reservations about marrying the guy at all. That she could blow hot and cold about the man she'd once intended to spend the rest of her life —

Goose bumps prickled her arms, and she ceased pacing.

What was that? *Had* intended?

'And?' she prompted Karin. 'You went to his apartment? Had he been to my house yet?' He should have. They'd had a date. Although, it wouldn't have been the first time he'd cancelled. 'Did he find the note?' She rubbed her neck.

'Yes, but — '

'Yes, he found it?'

'And, yes, I went there. But, Nikki, he wasn't, uh, open to what I had to say.'

'What do you mean?'

'Hang on. Another call's coming in.'

The signal flattened as Karin put her on hold. Nikki tapped her foot. Now she knew how sheep felt at shearing time — edgy as all get-out.

The signal clicked again, and Karin's voice broke through the poor connection. 'Sorry, that was Mrs. Bidwell. She phones a dozen times a day.'

Nikki didn't want to hear about Mrs. Bidwell. 'Karin — knock-knock — Royce? What are you trying to tell me?'

Her cousin sighed. 'All right. Nikki, I don't think Royce cares if you sleep with Alex Hart or not.'

'What?' Her brain screamed. 'He didn't buy the fake hookup?'

'No, I mean he . . . doesn't care. Nikki, I'm sorry. He said he enjoys the freedom he's found with you, and if you want to have a little pre-wedding fling in return, he'll allow it. Just this once.'

'He *what*? He'd *allow* it? This once?'

'He said you and he are perfect together in every way but one. But that he's found a way to deal with it. And then, oh Nikki, he hit on me.'

Her jaw seized. She'd kill him! Abstinence was supposed to make the fiancé yearn fondly — but not for other women.

'He touched my butt and tried to kiss me. Then . . . ' Karin's voice lowered ' . . . he asked me to sleep with him. Ugh, I couldn't get out of there fast enough.'

If Nikki heard any more, she'd puke. She dropped onto the chair, the phone slippery in her clammy hand. Her fiancé had hit on her maid of honor while *she* had the hots for their best man?

What kind of warped engagement was this? He couldn't possibly love her.

A wave of curious emotion washed over her.

Liberation, if she wasn't mistaken.

'Nikki?' Karin asked. 'Are you okay?'

'Um, yeah, just rattled.'

Royce didn't love her. Well, whoop-de-do. That he'd upset Karin made

Nikki want to *plow* him, but she didn't feel the keen bite of betrayal she would have expected. She didn't feel dejected or devastated by his actions, just foolish for having fallen for him in the first place. And gullible. And disillusioned.

She didn't need to take another magazine quiz to understand why. Reality crashed in on her.

Her fiancé didn't love her — what a profound relief.

Because she didn't love him, either.

9

Ooh-La-La

Rubbing her arms, Nikki tromped along the pebble-strewn lakeshore. Although the sun plumped high in the azure sky, the crisp spring breeze had climbed steadily in the hour since she'd left the Gotobeds' cabin. She should have worn a sweater over her T-shirt, but how was she to have anticipated that her phone call to Royce would send her scampering to the refuge of the shadow-dappled woods, where she'd withdrawn into a newfound shell of insecurities without Violet or Willie or Alex around to pity her?

She was only returning to her cabin now so Alex wouldn't worry.

Tennis shoes scrunching gravel, she lifted her face to the cool air. While her phone call to Karin had rattled her, the follow-up call to Royce had peeled her eyes wide open. That she'd wasted two years engaged to the jerk hurt. However, to learn the depths of her gullibility had proved downright degrading.

Royce was slime — and the worst kind of coward, backpedaling over what he'd said to Karin. Nikki was better off without the creep.

She trudged up the grassy slope to the cabin. The van sat empty with the hood shut. Hopefully, Willie had returned to his wife. Nikki couldn't face him.

Could she face Alex?

Inhaling deeply, she entered the cabin. Bernie slept on the couch, and Alex sat at the table in a chair facing the door, a farming journal from her grandfather's collection open in front of him. He'd occupied the same spot for hours at a time the last couple of days. The man's passion for history enthralled her, as did the affection inherent in his tone whenever he mentioned his family.

When he cared about something or someone, he didn't hold back. If he ever asked a woman to marry him, it would be because he loved the lucky girl — not because he wanted something from her.

He was one of the few people who accepted Nikki for who she was; who wasn't always trying to tempt or deceive her into becoming the person he wanted her to be.

'How did it go?' he asked.

'It went,' she said on her way into the kitchen. *Please don't follow me.* Shame for her idiocy wracked her, and she didn't want him discovering the extent of her naïveté. However, if he pressed, she'd pour out her soul. She wouldn't be able to help herself.

Thank God he must have recognized her need for solitude, because sounds of his chair scraping back reached her ears . . . then his retreating footsteps . . . and finally the creaking springs of a bed as he sat or reclined upon it.

Sighing, she gazed at Santos, hunkered

near his food bowl. She petted the dog, then refreshed his water and fed him. As Santos munched, she dug cold cuts out of the refrigerator for submarine sandwiches. She craved the busy work, and Alex would appreciate it. He liked her cooking.

Unlike some people, who'd rather eat restaurant food five nights a week.

She gathered margarine, mayonnaise, and mustard, and deposited the containers on the counter. Lettuce, tomato, onion, and half a green pepper followed. Her engagement ring mocked her as her hands flitted between the frozen loaf of crusty French bread and opening the deli packages she'd brought for Royce.

The scum!

She yanked off the ring so quickly, her knuckle throbbed. She'd chuck it across the room, but he wasn't worth the energy. She tossed it on the counter.

As the diamond bounced along Formica, the pressure in her chest lifted. For too long, she'd carried the weight of Royce Carbuncle's so-called love on her finger. She'd never have to wear the offending chunk of ice again.

She didn't even like the damn thing. The design was garish, not her style at all, but Royce's.

Like everything in her life. Royce's tastes. Royce's decisions. Nikki the numbskull had just followed along.

Luckily, even numbskulls could learn.

She heated the oven to thaw the bread. Santos's head remained buried in his food bowl. The everyday sounds of his strong canine jaws munching kibbles soothed her.

'Need any help?'

Alex.

She turned. He leaned against the doorframe, hands in the pockets of his ridiculously short, baggy pants. This morning, the gray boxers had been absent from the bathroom, which meant he wore them again.

Too bad. She rather liked imagining his things unclad.

Her skin prickled. Barely over an

hour ago, she'd broken off her engagement and already she lusted for another man.

Not any man, though. Alex Hart was one of a kind.

'I'm okay.' She tried a smile. 'I'm making lunch.'

His gaze drifted over her. 'Don't,' he said in a gruff voice.

Heart beating like a tom-tom, she placed the foil-wrapped bread on the stovetop. 'Don't what?'

'Pretend nothing's happened.' He shoved off the doorframe. 'I know you phoned Royce after you talked to Karin. When you went into the woods, Violet came and told me. She said you needed time alone, or I would have gone after you.' He stepped toward her. 'It took everything in me *not* to go after you, Nikki. When you came inside a minute ago, it took everything I have not to encroach on your space.' He pulled his hands out of his pockets, fingers splaying. 'I'm running out of willpower.' His gaze locked on her face.

Her pulse scattered. 'What else did Violet say?'

'That you'd talk when the time was right. But I can't stand to see you in pain, Nik. Tell me what the jackass said. I'll gladly throttle him for you.'

'I'm not sure I want to witness any bloodshed — '

'Nikki — '

'He's not coming.'

Alex's gaze darkened. 'Did he have an excuse?'

'Yep.' The carbuncle's duplicity knew no bounds. Similar to *her*, with her crazy kidnapping scheme. But at least she knew when to stop. 'Some fake crisis at the clinic.'

'Fake?' Alex echoed, and she nodded.

'That's not what he told Karin, but it sure as hell is what he told me. Granted, he didn't say *fake* crisis. He did want me to believe him. But he tried to hand me a real snow-job, Alex. He caked on the charm nice and thick.' Her face heated. 'Get this. He told Karin he didn't *care* if I had a pre-wedding fling. He told *me* he knew the note was a ploy to get him to take time off. 'A sexy little game,' he called it. Then he said he believed so strongly that you and I aren't fooling around — and that we never would — that he didn't even call you to find out if you were home! He droned on and on about how much he'd wanted to play out my sexual fantasies by coming after me. But he couldn't.'

'Because of this crisis?'

'Yeah.' She snorted. 'A real lame one. A rich patient who threw a tizzy when his receptionist tried to reschedule her appointment. He tossed in a power lunch with my father and the clinic's other two partners. One of them is due to retire soon. Did you know that? I didn't. And then Royce can slither right in there.' She wriggled her hand in imitation of a snake's movements — one far slimier than poor Lucy. 'Turns out that's why he asked me to marry him. The clinic employs three doctors besides Royce. All of them want to make partner. Being with me gives him an edge. He doesn't love me, Alex. He never has.'

Alex's hands fisted. 'He told you that?'

'He didn't have to. It was pretty easy to guess that love was never part of the equation for him.'

Or her.

She saw things so clearly now.

She'd fallen for Royce, but for the wrong reasons. That someone her parents approved of had wanted *her*, had tricked her into believing he *accepted* her, had sucked her in.

She'd allowed him to use her. What a weak-willed wimp.

'He hit on Karin, you know.' She jerked a hand. 'She told me. But when I asked him about it, he said *Karin* hit on *him*. The ass! After that, the conversation fell apart. I got ticked, he became defensive. And then he began *dictating* to me. He actually laid out his plans for our life.'

'Aw, Nik.' Alex stepped forward

again. 'I wanted to warn you — '

'Don't you dare apologize, Alex. I wasn't ready to listen. This was my screw-up, no one else's.' Her hands trembled. She wiped them on her jeans. 'We have the ideal arrangement, he said. We're lousy together in bed, you know. Well, Royce doesn't think *he's* lousy, just me. Not only that, but he's had 'an indiscretion or two,' as he put it. And he wants me to accept that it might happen again! Accept that he's *unfaithful!* Apparently, he thinks I'm too chicken — '

'Nikki, hey.' Alex's long legs swallowed the space between them. His strong arms curled around her, his solid chest . . . *right there*. Offering a haven for her to shelter in. A refuge of sinew and muscle and caring man.

As Santos's munching filled the small kitchen, Nikki curled her arms around Alex's waist. 'That's why he kept postponing setting the wedding date. If he made partner before the wedding, then he wouldn't have to marry me at all. But he said I shouldn't worry, that our marriage is still in the best interests of the practice. My 'sexy little game' helped him realize that.'

Beneath her head, Alex's chest muscles tensed. 'He thinks you'll go through with the wedding?'

'He thinks I'm too spineless to call it off, even though I told him we're through,' she said against the flannel barrier hoarding Alex's warmth. 'He thinks I won't risk disappointing my parents — yet *again*, as he loves to remind me. Then he said he wants me to return to Seattle as soon as possible so we can 'discuss our future rationally'.' She mimicked Royce's deep voice. 'His one concession is that we can get married whenever I want. I finally get what I *thought* I was after, and, you know, it doesn't feel so sweet. Yeah, we'd get married, Royce would give me every material thing I couldn't care less about, he'd make partner, and then we'd have this supposedly wonderful, *loveless*, rotten sex life together.'

She gazed up. 'I don't want that anymore, Alex.'

'You never did,' he replied, his voice both rough and gentle. His hands slid up her shoulders and rested on either side of her neck. His thumbs massaged her knotted muscles. 'You've always wanted love, Nik. That's been clear from the start.' His mouth curved. 'Okay, maybe not when I was tied up in the van, but shortly afterward.'

She smiled a little. Alex soothed her frazzled soul so easily. Being with Royce had always felt off-kilter, but having this man hold her felt like coming home.

'Clear to you and to me, maybe, but not clear to my fiancé. My *former* fiancé,' she amended.

Oh, Alex's hands, his touch. As the gentle onslaught continued, hot smoke swirled inside her.

'Alex, I'm embarrassed. I should have picked up on his signals. No wonder we haven't made love in ages. There's been no love to make.' Not for either of them.

Alex's hazel gaze softened. His fingers glided up her throat. 'Ah, Nik . . . '

'Don't pity me,' she whispered.

'This isn't pity. Royce is an ass.'

She inhaled. 'He said . . . I don't do it for him.'

'Then he's more than an ass. He's an imbecile.' Alex's thumbs stroked her jaw, and the smoke swirled hotter. 'You're beautiful, sexy, desirable. Don't let any man ever tell you otherwise.'

Her mouth dried, and her blood rushed. Carnal need danced in her veins. Forget Royce and the last humiliating couple of hours. She wanted now. She had to know.

'Do you think I'm desirable?' she whispered.

His eyebrows arched. 'You have to ask?'

'Then show me,' she murmured, heart racing. She could scarcely believe her daring. Why tap-dance around her feelings for Alex any longer? Her sham of an engagement lay shattered at her feet. She was free to love whom she wanted. Free to share her body with a man whose slightest touch thrilled her.

He sucked in a breath. 'Do you know what you're saying?'

'Yes. I want you to show me, Alex.'

'We shouldn't. You need time.'

'I need *you*.'

'*Nikki*.' His hands cradled her face, his touch like silk, pure magic. 'You're killing me.'

'Then show me.' She skimmed her hands up and down his broad back. 'I want to make love with you, Alex. I've never wanted another man this badly. Not even Royce. Only you.'

A low groan issued from his throat as his mouth came down on hers.

Finally.

A dizzying sweetness filled her. Greedily, she pressed her lips to his. Opening her mouth, she took him in. Velvet stroked velvet.

But she wanted more. She wanted him deeper.

His fingers gathered in the curls at

her nape. Then his hands slipped downward, his palms caressing her shoulders and arms. His fingers warm, possessive. Tingles emanated from every inch of skin and cotton T-shirt he touched.

Nikki breathed him in. Sweet saints above, she'd never experienced anything remotely this wonderful with Royce. This hot and sweet mesh of want and need mixing, swirling, burning.

The sensations swamped her, threatened to drown her — and she loved it. Loved how free she felt with him.

How foolish she'd been to believe she could force love where none existed. Love found one at its own pace. She knew that now.

Love had given her Alex.

She grappled for his shirt buttons, and the plastic discs and ancient threads popped. His chuckle rumbled in her mouth as their kiss softened.

Pulling away, she pushed the ruined shirt off his shoulders, down both his biceps . . . trapping his arms in the worn fabric. She smoothed her hands over his muscular chest.

'Nikki,' he whispered. 'Are you sure?'

Her tummy swooped. 'More than I've ever been about anything.' She kissed him. 'Make love with me, Alex.'

'You don't have to ask me three times.' He shrugged off the shirt, and it fell into a puddle on the floor. He scooped her into his arms and carried her out of the kitchen. 'Your place or mine?' he asked with a glance toward the beds.

'Mine,' she murmured. 'Rusty's sleeping on yours.'

He carried her over. 'I don't have protection,' he cautioned as he lowered her onto the quilt.

'In the nightstand drawer.' Here she'd thought she'd arrived prepared to jump her former fiancé's despicable bones, but fate and a certain history professor had surprised her.

'I'll keep that location in mind,' Alex mumbled in the moment before their mouths fused.

His tongue entwined with hers, and pure sensation drove through her. She wriggled her hips beneath his welcome weight. An approving groan sounded in his throat.

Alex clasped one of her hands between their bodies while they kissed, his thumb grazing the underside of her naked left ring finger.

He lifted his head. 'You took off your ring.' His husky voice rolled like gravel.

'It means nothing to me,' she whispered.

'Well, that's good. Otherwise, we shouldn't do this.'

'We wouldn't, Alex. I don't tango.'

'Tango?' He smiled.

'You know what I mean. I don't cheat.'

His gaze, suddenly serious, captured hers. He brushed curls off her forehead and then planted a kiss above her right eyebrow. 'I know.'

*   *   *

'Meowrrrr! Pffft!'

'Wroof! Ruff-ruff-ruff-yip!'

'Rusty, no! Bernie!'

Stirring in the bed, Alex slit open an eye. Nikki, clad in her skimpy panties and T-shirt, dashed around the cabin in pursuit of the Siamese and Chihuahua members of the Untrainable Trio.

Mmm. They'd made love twice before showering and crawling beneath the quilt to doze and cuddle. However, any more bouncing on Nikki's part and he'd be up for a third round.

'Playing tag?' he asked lazily.

'Lucy escaped! Rusty's after her!'

With Bernie in hot pursuit, Alex jumped out of bed. The dog miscalculated a turn and bonked against the piano, yelping. Rusty whipped a paw under the old upright, where the garter snake must have hidden. Nikki crouched on the floor, ass poking the air. She pushed away the cat and reached beneath the piano.

By the time Alex pulled on his boxers — no way was he exposing himself to

259

all those flying claws and paws and *fangs* — Bernie had recovered enough from the piano-whack to resume harassing Rusty. The cat skidded beneath the bed, scattering magazines out onto the plank floor. Bernie scooted after the feline, and a noisy battle ensued beneath the bed.

Only Santos sat still. The old dog hunched in the kitchen doorway, his big head lolling on his paws and his baggy eyes bleary.

Alex reached Nikki. 'Let me help.'

'I have her.' She retrieved the snake from beneath the piano. Standing, she examined Lucy.

'How did she escape?' Alex asked, touching Nikki's arm. 'Did she slither down the wall?'

'Maybe.' Nikki paused. 'I fed her before our shower, while you were in the outhouse. I guess I didn't reposition the screen lid properly. She probably dropped to the windowsill and then the chair.' Ignoring the ruckus of Rusty and Bernie fighting beneath the bed, she caressed the snake. 'She doesn't look hurt, but she's scared, poor baby.'

As she handled the hardy-looking garter, mellow warmth filled Alex. While her devotion to the critter was admirable, the solution was obvious. He smiled. 'We should return Lucy to the wild, Nik. If she's escaped her terrarium once, she's bound to do so again. She's no longer traumatized by Willie, honey.'

Nikki pouted. 'Maybe not, but Rusty did a number on her.'

'And your cat won't stop. Lucy belongs outdoors.'

'I know. I'll keep her a couple more hours to make sure she's okay.' She padded barefoot to the chair beneath Lucy's shelf and climbed up. In the light streaming in from the window, her rear peeked out from her lace-edged panties.

God help me. He wanted that rear in his hands again . . .

He shifted his feet on the cool floor. What a fool he was, indulging in erotic fantasies while she cared for Lucy. He didn't want her feeling like he only wanted her for sex. Royce had put her through the wringer enough already.

Speaking of the hairball, where had his former pal gotten off insinuating Nikki was frigid? She was the most giving and responsive lover Alex had ever known.

Granted, he'd lived like a monk these past few months, but he had a memory, and no woman within that memory held a candle to her.

Hell, she even had him thinking in clichés.

He allowed his gaze to travel up her slender legs as she stretched on tiptoe to lower Lucy into the vivarium.

Making love with his angel-haired wood nymph had recharged his emotions as well as his libido. He loved her, and he wanted the best for her. But was the 'best' him? Continually hot for her beautiful body while she struggled with the disintegration of her dream of a future with Royce?

He'd caught her watching how affectionate and fun the Gotobeds were together, and he'd listened while she'd talked about the differences between her parents' practical marriage and her grandparents' loving union. Like Violet and like her own grandmother, Nikki deserved a man who would always, unfailingly, be there for her. A help-mate. A life partner. Not a zit doctor with his nose firmly shoved up his rich patients' behinds.

And, very possibly, not some burned-out history professor tired of the soulless politicking that accompanied the climbing of the ivory tower.

Jaw ticking, he turned to tidy the magazines strewn on the floor between the beds. Nikki had read dozens of them over the last couple of days, often with pen in hand. Doing crossword puzzles, she'd said whenever he'd asked.

As he crouched to fetch the first magazine, Rusty streaked out from under the bed, knocking open the tattered pages. The cat darted for the refuge of the storage boxes, Bernie zipping after him.

Alex picked up the magazine and skimmed the age-dulled page. A faded red heading announced: *Dig Him or Dump Him? How to Tell if He's 'The One.'*

Someone had scribbled answers to the multiple-choice quiz in the margins. Two sets — one labeled 'R' and the other 'A.'

He frowned. *'R' for Royce and 'A' for . . . him?*

Nikki had compared them?

He scanned the questions, mainly sexual in tone.

Suddenly, the magazine was wrenched out of his hands.

10

Afterglow, Afterglow, Where Art Thou?

'Nikki, what — ?'

'I'll get these,' she said, sweeping past him and bending between the beds. She scooped the remaining magazines into her arms. As she straightened, the pages of the one she'd grabbed from him flapped at the bottom of her messy load. 'I know I'm a slob at times, but you don't have to clean for me, Alex.'

'You're not a slob.' But obviously hiding something from him. *Crossword puzzles, my foot.*

He stepped toward her, and she backed against the nightstand.

'How to tell if *who's* the one?' he asked.

'*Who* who?' Her eyebrows lifted in poorly feigned ignorance. With her curls in disarray from their cuddling and her face scrubbed clean from their shower, she looked both adorably innocent and sexy.

A top magazine slipped, and she snatched it back into place. Two others thumped onto the plank floor.

'Who *you* know who,' Alex said. 'I don't.' Although he'd guessed. 'That's why I'm asking.'

'Who who's on first?'

'What?'

'No, he's on second. Or is that third?' She giggled, a blush tingeing her cheeks.

Another magazine slipped, dangling from her elbow. Alex caught it as it fell. He flipped a doggy-eared page. The headline greeted: *Separating the Studs from the Slugs — A Single Girl's Guide to Weeding out Creeps*. A breezy-toned article followed.

He turned the next page. Another quiz this time. As before, two columns had been scribbled in the margins, tallying two sets of answers: *A* and *R*.

He tossed the magazine onto her bed

and picked up the two from the floor. A quick perusal of each revealed similarly toned articles and quizzes.

'Nikki, what's going on?' He didn't mind the content of the magazines, but the manner in which she'd used them — and then lied about it. Was she more mixed up about Royce, and therefore probably about *him*, than he'd realized?

'Nothing.' The remaining magazines in her arms shifted. 'Just passing the time.'

'By taking quizzes?' Alex asked beneath the din of Rusty and Bernie racing around the storage boxes.

'Why not?'

'Because, correct me if I'm wrong, these quizzes say you're confused.'

She blinked those huge baby blues. 'You're wrong.'

'Excuse me?'

Her chin hoisted. 'You said to correct you if you're wrong. You are.' She tightened her grip on her tilting armload.

'Sure, I am. And, any second now,

Royce will barge in to 'rescue' you. Your word, Nikki, not mine.' Uttered less than a week ago.

'That's not fair.'

'I'm sorry. But, Nikki, the first time we had sex today, near the end, you whispered that you love me.' Although the softly spoken words had thrilled him, he'd assumed they were driven by her passion. Nikki wore her emotions proudly. However, in the throes of their activities, she might have mistaken her physical release with love.

A smile curved her mouth. 'I do . . . love you,' she whispered.

His chest knotted. There it was again, her uncertainty, her hesitation. She might not recognize it, but he did.

He pointed out, 'More precisely, Nik, you said you *thought* you loved me.'

'I did?' She shook her head. 'Well, now I definitely know I do.'

'Because we had sex a second time?' He glanced at the quiz questions in the top magazine he held. 'Because it was 'mind-blowing'? Sex isn't love, Nik. No matter how great it feels.'

Hurt flashed on her face, and a steel band gripped his chest. He'd often delivered the same speech to his impressionable sisters, when some guy promising one of them the moon and stars had broken her heart instead. Now it dawned on him that Nikki, at twenty-five, was one year younger than Cassie and three years younger than Sarah.

And six years younger than him.

Those six years immediately gaped wider than the Grand Canyon.

Alex tossed the two magazines onto his bed. Technically, six years between adults wasn't a huge difference. His father had eight years on his mom, and they shared a closeness he envied — and craved for himself.

Yet, when paired with Nikki's naïveté, those six years gained in significance. He'd always realized she trusted too easily. Damn it, he should have known better than to make love to her while she was vulnerable.

'Nikki, I don't want to hurt you — '

'But you have.' Her features hardened. 'Sex isn't love? I can't believe you said that. Alex, don't you think I've learned anything? This past week has been very illuminating. Royce and I had sex every once in a while, and what I felt for him was nothing, *nothing* like what I feel for you.'

'But you thought it was. Until a few hours ago, you were convinced you loved him.'

'I wasn't convinced I loved him so much as I was desperate to believe our engagement wasn't a lie. That he hadn't made a fool out of me.'

Oh Nikki. 'You can say that now that you know he used you. But, sweetheart, when you first brought me here, it certainly seemed like you loved him.'

'Okay, so I *was* confused. That's past tense, Alex.'

'You're not confused now?'

She shook her head. The sunlight streaming in from the windows glimmered off her silvery-blonde curls, lending her the appearance of a disheveled and disappointed angel.

And he was the jerk who'd burst her bubble of romantic illusions.

'Nikki . . . honey . . . ' He gestured to the magazines clutched against her chest. 'Given all the R's and A's on those pages, how can you say you're not confused?'

'Alex, I *told* you. Maybe I was confused when I did the tests, but I'm not anymore. And it has nothing to do with you and me making love. I was on the verge of realizing I couldn't marry Royce before I phoned Karin. That's why I was so jumpy this morning. Every time you came near me, I wanted to touch you. I wanted to tell you how I felt. But I couldn't, not while I was engaged. I *had* to contact Royce. I had to let him explain, to find out what went wrong with my plan. Not because I loved him, but because I felt some warped sense of duty toward him, I suppose.'

Alex sighed. 'You suppose?'

'Oh my God. After what we've shared, you can ask that?'

'I can ask that *because* of what we've shared, Nikki.' Gut burning, he turned and strode out from between the beds. Bernie whimpered near the back door, while Rusty, hunched atop a stack of cardboard boxes, bared his fangs and hissed at the little dog. 'Hell, Nik, I made love with you maybe ninety minutes after you broke up with Royce. I didn't give you a chance to think. I didn't allow you a chance to *heal*.'

'You gave me a chance.'

'Not enough of one.'

'Maybe I didn't want one.' She chucked the load of magazines onto her bed. One bounced and flipped off the other side. Bernie yelped as it landed near the boxes.

'I should have given it to you, anyway.' Alex rubbed his face. 'Look, I know what you're going through. I've seen this sort of thing happen with my sisters. You came to me — no, worse, you made love with me — on the rebound. And I let it happen.'

'Give me some credit, Alex. How can I rebound from an engagement that never truly existed? No. I asked you to make love with me because I — ' she jabbed her chest repeatedly ' — Nikki St. James, being of sound mind and a damn horny body, *wanted* to.'

Her cleavage jiggled from the force of the jabbing. Man, how he'd like nothing better than to toss his sense of right and wrong out the window and pull her into his arms again. Make love with her until he didn't know where either of them began or ended.

But he couldn't close the chasm he'd created without costing her the time and space she needed.

'You asked me if you were desirable.' The words scratched in his throat.

'Because I wanted to know if *you* thought I was. Because I wanted *you*. And still do. I want you, Alex.'

'And I want you. Damn it, I'm struggling here, Nikki. I love you, too. But I need to feel extremely sure that

273

you know what you want. If we became a couple now, who's to say you'd be truthful about your needs? That you wouldn't sacrifice your goals to mine? You said that's what you did with Royce, and what you've always done with your family. I couldn't take it if you lost yourself in me, too.'

'But I know what I want.' Her voice broke.

'You *think* you want me, Nikki. Just like you thought you loved Royce. We've been isolated in this cabin for five nights.' Quickly approaching six if he stayed. 'That's a mighty short time frame during which to change your mind about something that will affect the rest of your life.'

A humorless laugh shot from her. 'Just because a person changes her mind quickly doesn't mean it's not a valid change! You talk about *me* not knowing what I want. How I've given up my dreams for others.' She clapped her chest. 'And I admit it. I have. But you'd better look in a mirror, Alex, because something tells me you're not too clear about what you want, either. You seem pretty unhappy working at PU, so why keep teaching there?'

He swore. 'This isn't about me, Nik.' He reached for the clothes on his bed.

'It's about both of us.'

'I don't want to hear it.' He had to make a break now — for her. Before she convinced him otherwise. 'What you need is time, and I've stolen that from you.'

'So then what do you propose we do, Kemosabe?'

He yanked on the baggy pants and old shirt. 'I have to go.'

'Now? Where?'

'Back to Seattle.' He located a couple of dangling buttons and swiftly latched them. 'Violet and Willie are close by, if you need them. And the van is running again, so I'm not stranding you without transportation.'

She flung up a hand. 'You're still leaving?'

Cinching his belt, he pushed bare

feet into his loafers. 'I don't have a choice. You need time to think about what's happened with Royce; about what you want to do with your life. What kind of man would I be if I didn't allow you that time?'

She snorted. 'So you'll hitchhike back to Seattle and bury yourself in some dusty library again?'

He didn't expect her to understand that he had her best interests at heart. 'If I have to.' Before she could say or do anything to change his mind, he grabbed his laptop case and wallet and strode out the back door.

★ ★ ★

Mouth dropping open, Nikki stood between the beds in her panties and T-shirt. He'd left her. Alex had actually left her!

She jammed her hands on her hips. Of all the lowdown, patronizing choices he could have made! He'd made love with her — not once but twice — then claimed he had to leave her for her own good. She'd suffered years of her parents and Royce dictating what was best for her, and now she had to endure the same nonsense from Alex?

She had half a mind — no, make that a full mind — to run into the woods with the leftover rope and duct tape, sneak ahead of him before he traveled too far on the rutted road, and ambush him.

Jump him from behind and wrestle him to the ground. Leave him hogtied until he saw reason.

If necessary, she'd resort to the pillowcase and blindfold. She'd even set Bernie on him — except the traitorous dog now adored the man. But what else could she do? Race after him half-naked?

Yeah, that made zero sense.

She glanced around for her jeans. A low moan from across the cabin reached her ears, and she lifted her gaze. In the kitchen entrance, Santos struggled to his feet. His big head lolled between his shoulders, the drool stringing from his muzzle was thicker and longer than normal. His pleading brown eyes located her — and he heaved.

'Santos?' She hurried to the dog. 'Are you sick, boy?' But why? She whipped her head to the kitchen counter. Not one single cold cut remained.

'Santos!' She crouched in front of him. 'You know you can't eat that much meat! On a full belly, to boot!' She sobbed. Why had she left those open deli packets on the counter? 'There, there, fella. It'll be okay. Let it come. Don't fight it.' She massaged his scruff.

Santos moaned. While he barfed onto the floor, Nikki fetched a small garbage bag and the roll of paper towels. She returned to find her pet lying on his side, a short distance from the vomit. During the past few minutes, Bernie had escaped from the cat. Whining, the little dog nosed Santos's head.

Nikki petted and cooed to the Saint Bernard. 'Feeling better, boy?' On her knees, she cleaned up the doggy vomit with the paper towel, and her hand hit a sharp object. Bones always made Santos barf, but where had he found one?

She picked up the bone with a fresh chunk of toweling. Through the dripping muck, a familiar diamond glittered.

'My ring?' Eyes wide, she looked at the dog. 'Santos, you ate my ring! Poor baby, no wonder you're sick!' She laughed, although it wasn't funny. Thank heavens the ring had emerged from Santos's . . . front end.

She carried the dripping ring to the sink. She rinsed and dried the ring, then tossed it into a cupboard for safekeeping. Tears burned her eyes.

Damn it, she couldn't chase after Alex now. Santos might puke again. Considering the huge amount of deli meat the old dog had consumed, she couldn't guarantee he'd continue using his front end. She'd spend the afternoon caring for the ailing animal outdoors.

She returned to the dogs and resumed cleaning the barf.

Minutes later, she found her jeans under a bed. As she tugged them on, a knock sounded at the back door, and her heart leapt. Had Alex realized his mistake and returned?

Zipping the jeans, she ran to the door and opened it. Violet stood on the other side, holding a pan of brownies. The rich, moist scent of decadent chocolate wafted from the treat, and an understanding smile graced Violet's face. The kind woman's visit couldn't make up for Alex's absence, though.

Nikki's shoulders drooped.

He'd really left.

Violet's gaze traveled over Nikki's hot cheeks. 'Oh dear,' the old woman murmured. 'It's as I feared. Alex has upset you, hasn't he?'

Blowing out a breath, Nikki stepped aside.

As Violet entered, she extended the pan of brownies. Rusty hopped down from the storage boxes and wound between the woman's legs. 'Here you are, dear,' Violet said. 'I baked these for Willie, then decided you might need them more. Be careful when you eat them, though. There's a crushed Rise-All tablet in . . . that one.' She pointed at a square in the middle.

'Thank you.' Closing the door, Nikki accepted the warm pan. 'But you don't have to give me Willie's brownies.'

'Of course I do. Friends comfort one another.'

Nikki stared at the pan. 'Violet, I love Alex. He thinks I can't, because it happened quickly, but I do.'

The old lady patted Nikki's shoulder. 'I know, dear. If it makes you feel better, I believe he loves you, too. He came to see Willie and me before he left, you know. He asked us to keep an eye on you. Dense as the man might be about the workings of the female heart, would he do that if he didn't love you?'

'I don't know.' Alex had said he loved her. Rather, he'd practically shouted it.

Had he meant it or had he been trying to placate her?

She carried the brownies to the nightstand and set them down. A glance toward Santos revealed the dog sleeping near the kitchen, where she'd left him. Bernie napped beside his canine brother. Good, she had some time with Violet before Santos became nauseous again.

She sat on the edge of the bed, and Violet settled beside her. Rusty jumped up and curled in a ball behind them.

Violet said, 'Willie insisted on driving Alex to town so your young man could rent a car. Alex wanted to ride that rickety kid's bike to the highway and then hitchhike to town wearing those scraggly clothes. Can you imagine? His shirt is missing half its buttons!'

Willie. Nikki narrowed her eyes. *The turncoat.*

'Why would Willie drive him? Does he think Alex was right to leave?'

'Well, it's like this, dear. Aside from the fact that Alex could very well damage his baby-making capabilities by riding a too-small bike down a bumpy dirt road, Willie understands your young man believes he's doing right by you.'

Not that again. 'Do *you* believe Alex is doing right by me?'

The old woman's gaze didn't waver. 'Perhaps dear, I realize you love him. I don't think you *think* you love him, like he thinks. I feel with all my heart that you do. I've known you since you were a toddler, after all. Although we haven't seen one another in years, I still feel close to you. In some ways, talking to you is like talking to your grandmother. And you know how highly I thought of her.'

'Aw, Violet.' Nikki squeezed her friend's hand.

'Hush, let me finish. I remember falling in love with my Willie . . . the spark, the confusion, then the knowing. Oh, child, the joyful knowing. However, from what you've told me about your engagement to that Royce person,

I also believe that perhaps you've only recently discovered what true love is. And you've found it with Alex.'

Nikki's heart lifted. Violet understood!

'But you have to give the poor man time, dear. Consider things from his point of view. You've turned his life topsy-turvy. Remember, he's just a man. A wonderful specimen, yes, but at the mercy of his maleness. The poor boy's head is spinning. He needs to collect himself. To gather his reserves, so to speak. He has to believe he's in some sort of control, even though we both realize he isn't.'

A smile tugged Nikki's mouth. 'Violet . . . are you saying *I* don't need time, but that Alex does?'

'Frankly, you both could benefit from a little breather.' Violet chuckled. 'Nikki, you might know what you want, but your young man still has to accept that you do. So, let him.'

Let him. What a novel concept.

'How?'

'Well, first you have to give him what he thinks you need . . . '

Time. Nikki grinned. 'And then I knock his socks off.'

11

Making a New Bed

'Nikki, are you sure about this?' Karin asked from behind the wheel of the van idling at the curb of Royce's upscale condo complex. 'Confronting Royce seems a bit risky.'

Nikki arched her eyebrows. Karin was her family, her best friend, and, in tonight's case, her get-away driver. However, sometimes Nikki's cousin required . . . persuading. 'Kare, what do you think will happen? That my knees will soften like pudding at the first sight of the carbuncle and I'll fall for him again?'

'It hasn't been very long — '

'Since I dumped his sorry butt? It's been a week.' People and their relation-ship schedules! What about the only one of importance?

286

Seven tortuous days had passed since Alex had walked out on her at Lake Eden, and that hurt more than anything Royce had ever done. One hundred sixty-eight-and-counting hours had elapsed in excruciating slow-motion since Violet had counseled her over and over ... since Nikki had drawn on every drop of patience at her disposal not to race back to Seattle and deal with Royce *and* Alex lickety-split.

'Besides, I'm not confronting Royce, per se,' she assured her cousin. 'I have to see him tonight, whether I want to or not — ' and she most assuredly did not wish to see him ' — so Alex will believe me when I explain, yet again, that Royce and I are through.' Totally trashed. Face-to-face finished. No wimping out with cell phone calls or social network status updates or a scribbled note shoved beneath her former fiancé's door.

'But he's such a jerk.' Karin's eyes flashed. 'I can say that now. I couldn't bear to disillusion you before.' She paused as the old van rumbled and shook the seats. 'Although maybe I should have. Nikki, if I'd told you how I felt about Royce from the start . . . '

'Would I have listened?' Nikki sighed. 'I was a different person when he and I met. My entire life revolved around what others thought of me and what they wanted for me.' And *from* her. 'Not anymore.'

'But you and Alex happened so fast.'

Yeah, yeah. 'That's why I'm slowing it down.' In the end, she'd still get what she wanted — she hoped. Alex Hart, beside her, for the rest of her life. 'Now, where are those brownies?' She fetched her purse off the floor mat.

Karin reached behind the driver's seat and passed Nikki the pan of brownies Violet had baked at Lake Eden last Wednesday. The pan had sat on Nikki's cabin counter for two days before she'd stashed the treat in the tiny refrigerator freezer. Without Alex to share them with, Violet's gift had nearly gone to waste. However, half an hour ago, Nikki had reheated the brownies in her oven at home, and they once more smelled as fresh and delicious as if Violet had baked them this morning.

Royce would love them. Especially the middle one.

'Thanks for supporting me tonight.' Leaning across the seats with the brownies in hand, Nikki hugged her cousin. 'Circle the block until I return. The doorman is zapping us the hairy eyeball.'

Karin smiled. 'We are in a no-parking zone.'

Saying goodbye to her cousin, Nikki climbed out of the passenger side and stared at the fourteen-story building. Royce lived on the twelfth floor — as close to the top as his bank account permitted. He'd promised that after the wedding they would move to a townhouse which accepted pets. And she, like a patsy, had believed him. She'd pored over the real estate listings for months, but nothing she liked had matched Royce's taste.

And she'd believed that, too. *What a dunce.*

Minutes later, after chatting up the doorman, she rode the elevator and disembarked. She carried the brownies down the hall and knocked on El Carbuncle's door. 'Royce? It's me.' Right on time. When she'd called this afternoon to arrange to see him, he'd sounded delighted. Positively gleeful. The five-foot-nine-inch twerp.

'One minute!' his twerpish voice announced from inside.

Nikki's stomach cramped. She closed her eyes. *You can do this. You have to. Without barfing all over his carpet.*

He opened the door in the midst of tucking in his shirt. 'I took a shower,' he said in a suggestive tone. A crooked smile tilted his lips, and his eyebrows waggled: Carbuncle code for *You're Finally Going to Get Lucky Again*. He ran a hand through his damp hair.

Nikki snorted. 'Not gonna happen.'

'But you asked to see me. Haven't you come to your senses?'

'Ohhh, yes.'

'I thought so.' His gaze softened. 'Nikki, come in. We'll talk this out.' He opened the door wide, but she stood her ground.

'We can talk here.'

'Come on, Nikki.' He ran a thumb along his lower lip.

Was this his new sexy look? It sucked.

'I said no.'

He grunted. 'Why bring me brownies then?'

'They're a goodbye gift.' His favorite snack. He'd gobble them the minute she left. 'It's a new recipe. The center square is the chewiest.' She shoved the pan into his hands.

He glanced at the brownies. 'But you have to come back to me. We were great together — '

''In every way but one,'' she quoted from his encounter with Karin.

He glowered at her. 'Your cousin was lying.'

'Don't give me that.'

Holding the pan in one hand, he

lifted the other. 'Okay, forget I said a word to her. I was upset.'

Nikki batted her eyelashes. 'I don't care.'

'Yes, you do.' The glower returned. 'Your father will never accept the kind of guy who'd be into you, Nikki. Who'd fall for your ditzy hot blonde routine only to discover you're frigid.'

Red-hot fury boiled inside her. She slapped his face. Hard.

'Ow!' He rubbed his cheek. 'What was that for?'

'Figure it out.'

'You made your bed with me, Nicole — '

'That doesn't mean I have to sleep in it!' She dug into her purse. The glitzy engagement ring she hadn't worn in a week cut into her palm. 'What happens between me and my parents is no longer your business. Neither is my sex life.' She jammed the ring into the middle brownie. Now he'd have to dig it out. He'd probably lick it off.

Excellent. With luck, a side effect

would kick in and he'd suffer ten hours of torture.

He poked the brownie. 'I'll still make partner.'

'Bully for you.' Gripping her purse, she hurried to the elevator. The clever carbuncle didn't follow.

Inside, she watched the numbers as the compartment whisked her back to the lobby. Her heart beat like she'd mainlined forty lattes, and her spirit soared like a young swallow frolicking on a spring breeze.

She was her own woman now. Really her own woman, for the first time ever. No matter what happened with Alex over the next few weeks, she was in charge of her future.

Starting tonight.

* * *

Alex checked behind the huge rhododendron bush like he had every soul-eroding day in the five weeks since he'd left Nikki at Lake Eden. And, as on each of those dreary afternoons, his mood deflated at what he found: zilch. No kooky blonde waiting to ambush him. No ropes, no toy ray gun, no fake-teenage-boy voice issuing crazy threats.

No Nikki.

What else had he expected after the way he'd treated her?

Unlocking his apartment door, he entered the kitchen and placed his laptop case on the dinette table. His first day teaching PU's second summer session had proceeded smoothly. The Early American History seminar boasted a handful of students, although a couple were playing catch-up with undergrad programs. The rest appeared eager to learn, which would render his ivory-tower swan song easier to endure.

September would find him teaching at a small college. Thanks to Nikki telling him to examine his own life, he'd been short-listed by two Eastern Washington schools.

The move would allow him to focus on teaching while situating him closer to his parents and sisters in Idaho. *But hundreds of miles from Nikki.*

Damn. He paced back and forth for several moments. He hated putting almost an entire state between them, but he needed the distance. Remaining in Seattle would prove too great a temptation. He'd already dropped into Dr. Green's vet clinic — after borrowing his landlords' iguana and calling ahead with a fake name to ensure Nikki had the day off — to soak up some wood-nymph ambience. And what about the night he'd sat in his car outside her rental house for three hours, hoping to catch a glimpse of her through the blinds . . . and feeling like a borderline stalker?

Resolved not to confuse her again by barging back into her life and taking over — like Royce and her parents had always done, like he'd done more than once with his sisters, hell, like he'd done with Nikki before abandoning her at the cabin — he hadn't knocked on her door.

Over the last five weeks, he hadn't contacted her.

And she hadn't contacted him.

Her message rang loud and clear. She'd realized she didn't love him — and she never had.

A hollow sensation gaped inside him.

After toeing off his shoes, he retrieved two cartons of Thai take-out from the fridge. Sitting at the table, he plunged a fork into the cold noodles. He couldn't avoid Nikki forever. Much as it would kill him to witness her change of I-love-Alex-Hart, he needed to see her before he left Seattle.

Hopefully, in a crowded, noisy coffee shop, she wouldn't feel pressured or patronized by his presence. Or by the desire showing in his eyes, his voice, and every gesture.

He crunched a peanut, then stabbed another forkful of noodles. A coward might choose not to see her at all. But he couldn't — and didn't want to — do that. On top of the burning urgency to be near her *just one more time*, he had a lot to thank her for. As feeble as that sounded.

A mere six days with Nikki had opened his mind to the unfulfilling path his life had taken. All these years, he'd driven himself ceaselessly toward tenure — for what? Yeah, he wanted job security as much as the next guy. However, he would rather connect with his students on a daily basis. Who needed the energy-draining politics of achieving tenure at warp speed?

What surprised him most was his candid phone call to his parents about his epiphany — and their reaction. They preferred that he teach at a small college! So he could 'get a life' outside academia, his mother had remarked.

He'd been so wrong to assume his family *wanted* him to reach for the brass ring. *Just like you assumed what Nikki needed*. And then had forced it upon her, despite her protests.

You're an idiot, Hart.

Maybe, if he went to her right now and begged forgiveness for acting the schlep, she'd give him another chance. Grabbing his car keys, he leapt off his chair.

A knock rapped on the door.

What now?

He pocketed the keys and opened the door to a carrot-haired delivery guy hefting a huge parcel.

'Alex Hart?' the young man inquired. 'Sign here.' He extended a digital gadget.

As Alex scrawled his signature, a Siamese cat winding around the delivery guy's legs gazed up at him and meowed.

Alex shook his head. 'Rusty?'

The cat yawned, exposing toothless gums. '*Meowrr!*'

'Cat yours?' The guy retrieved the device. ''cause it followed me from the sidewalk.' He handed over the parcel and hustled off.

Alex stared at the cat. 'Rusty, what are you doing here?' Glancing around the corner of the house, he peered toward the parking area. No white van.

He looked at the cat again. Was he dealing with a Rusty clone wandering the neighborhood, or the real thing? But if the cat was Rusty, how had he gotten here? Had he stowed away in the delivery van?

Which then begged the question, was the parcel from Nikki?

The Rusty look-alike meowed again and sauntered into the apartment. Alex scanned the parcel label. The big package *was* from Nikki. What had she sent him?

'Wrrr-ooof! Yip, yip, yip-yip-yap!'

Bernie — the real enchilada, there couldn't be two of the Rambo wannabes — zipped through the open door, the late June air riffling in his wake. Something was definitely up.

'Woof!' A baritone bark preceded Santos's entrance. Saint Bernard drool splattered the linoleum before Santos joined Rusty and Bernie in the living room. The Untrainable Trio variously sat or stood on Alex's wood-laminate floor and watched him.

All right, *maybe* he could buy Bernie and Rusty as stowaways, but Santos? No way could the delivery guy have missed a hulking Saint Bernard in his van.

Alex plunked the parcel on the table and strode back to the open door. A curly-haired blonde in white jeans and a yellow T-shirt knotted at her midriff breezed past him. Her silver belly-button ring glinted.

Alex blinked. Backed up. Lifted his head. And blinked for a second time at the beautiful sight of Nikki's sparkling blue eyes.

With her animals rolling out the red carpet ahead of her, her appearance made sense . . . and yet it didn't.

Why would she come here? And what for?

Maybe she travels light, Hart. Maybe everything she owns is in that parcel, and she's moving in.

Wishful thinking.

She smiled. 'Hi, Alex.' She wriggled her fingers at the Trio. 'Good fellas.'

He collected his thoughts, organized his tongue. 'I meant to call you.' *You're a lame-ass, Hart.*

'I saved you the trouble.' She sailed to the dinette table. 'You received my package.'

He closed the door. 'It just arrived.'

'I know. I followed the delivery van over here.'

Don't try to figure her out, Hart. Go with the Nikki-flow.

'You did?'

'Yep. I parked out front.' She plopped her purse onto the crowded table. 'I wanted to surprise you.'

The fog slowly lifted from his brain. He tucked his hands into his pants pockets. 'Well . . . you've succeeded.'

She beamed. 'Good. Alex, I've missed you so much! This last month has been awful.'

'It has?' *Geez, could you sound any stupider?*

'I loved you five weeks ago, and I love

301

you now. Nothing's changed for me, professor.'

'You're not confused?'

'I never was.'

'Then why did you wait — '

'Because you were.'

'*I* was confused?'

'Maybe.' Her lips twitched with another smile. 'Or maybe you needed time instead of me. That's why I didn't come see you before today. I can't take all the credit for waiting. It was Violet's idea.'

'Figures.' Alex chuckled. Then just stood there drinking in the sunshiny vision that was Nikki.

Was she really here? With him? Saying she still loved him?

She had a point about him needing time. He hadn't understood that while they were at the cabin. Thinking back, though, what she said made a Nikki sort of sense.

In the span of six days, she'd spun his life into so many new and refreshing directions that maybe he'd needed to catch his breath.

Ruts were damn difficult to escape. But he had one foot on solid ground. With Nikki's help, he'd soar out the rest of the way.

He stepped toward her. 'You love me, and there's no confusion?'

She shook her head. 'Nope.'

'Fancy that, Miss St. James, because nothing's changed for me, either. Nothing to do with how I feel about you, anyway.'

'And what way would that be?' Her head tilted.

'The way I felt about you at the cabin — and still do. I love you, Nik. Every kooky, zany, delicious inch of you.'

'Then stop moving at a snail's pace, Hart. Scoot your buns on over here and kiss me.'

He obliged. Gathered her into his arms and pressed his mouth to hers. Inhaled her springtime scent, the hope and joy she breathed into him.

When Santos barked, they came up for air.

'Mmm.' Cupping Nikki's face, Alex kissed the tip of her nose. They had a lot to discuss. But first . . . 'What did you bring me?' At this rate, it wouldn't surprise him if Lucy slithered out of the parcel.

She glanced at the package. 'Two pairs of pants, as promised, to replace the pair I ruined. And my grandfather's farming journals. They were my excuse to come over here. In case things didn't work out between us, I planned to leave the journals and take off.'

Aw, hell. He'd caused her as much pain as he'd experienced these last five weeks.

He placed his hands on her shoulders. 'You didn't need to replace my pants, Nik.'

'I wanted to. I forgot to buy the new shirts, though.' Her forehead puckered.

'Don't worry about the shirts. Tell me about the journals.'

'They're getting destroyed at the cabin. It's too drafty, and the lake air isn't good for them. I'd like to donate them. Do you have any ideas who could use them?'

'Definitely.' One of the colleges that had interviewed him boasted substantial archives. 'Are you sure you want to part with them?'

She nodded. 'I adored my grandfather, but I carry his memory with me.' She patted her chest, above her heart. 'Right here. Same place I carry you.' Her soft smile filled him with a warm glow. 'When I watched you reading the journals, I realized Gramps would have loved the thought of donating them. But you have the connections. I don't.'

He slid a hand down her arm, fingers gliding along her smooth skin. 'Um, yeah. Nikki, I have to tell you something.'

Her gaze remained glued to his. 'What? Don't worry, whatever it is, I can take it. I won't crumple into a ball and die.'

He believed her. 'I'm leaving Seattle,' he said, rubbing her arms. 'You were right when you said I'm not happy at

PU. I submitted my paper, and I'll teach the second summer session because I made the commitment, but after that I'm moving closer to Idaho and taking a posting at a small college. At least, that was the plan, until you showed up. Now I don't know if I want to follow through with it.'

Her gaze brightened. 'Alex, you have to follow through! How close to Idaho are you moving?'

'Probably Pullman, if everything works out.'

She wiggled. 'Perfect! When do you leave?'

Now she *wanted* him to leave her? He'd never figure her out, but he'd love to spend his life trying.

'Summer session ends the beginning of August, so sometime after that.'

She laughed. Bright, tinkling bubbles that started both dogs barking — and Rusty meowing.

'I'm moving in August, too!'

Come again? 'You're moving?'

'Yes! You said I needed to think about

what I want to do with my life, and so I did. I stayed at the cabin a few days, set Lucy free, and just thought. Well, and fished with Willie. The answer came to me nearly right away, but I wanted to 'make sure,' like you said, so I kept fishing, drank tons of tea with Violet, returned to work at the vet clinic, and then thought some more.'

Alex smiled. 'Where did all this thinking lead?' He slid his hands up and down her arms again.

'Vet school. I'm really going, Alex! I'm checking out a number of schools, but I'm hoping for Washington State in Pullman. The admission deadline for this September has passed, but applications for next fall will be online in a few months. I'm visiting the campus next week and finding an apartment.' She bounced in his arms. 'My boss introduced me to a friend of his there. Not for the apartment, for a job. I'll work at her clinic until I start WSU next year. Isn't that exciting?'

He nodded . . . through another

daze. She'd knocked him for a loop. Again. And he never wanted her to stop.

Without Nikki, his life crumbled like dry bread. But with her, through her, he'd learned how to feed his soul again.

She fed his soul.

She was a precious gift, and he didn't want to lose her.

'What did your parents say?' he asked.

'Oh Alex! You won't believe this. I hardly believe it myself. I went to see them the same night I saw Royce. I wanted to return his ring first . . . and give him some stale brownies Violet baked.' She giggled. 'Then I went to Mother and Father and told them — note, I didn't ask their permission, I *told* them — this is what I'm doing. Ditching that cheating slime Royce and becoming a vet. If you love me, you'll stand by me.'

'No kidding.' She'd asserted herself with her family and lived to tell the tale.

Without pulling stunts, without pretending she majored in Art History, without wrapping the senior St. Jameses in duct tape and kidnapping them, she'd done it. 'And?'

'They approved! It took a lot of talking — poor Karin waited in the van for an hour before we could go out and celebrate — but all this business with Royce has changed things for my parents and me. Once Father realized how dishonest Royce is, he said, and I quote, 'The pimple will never get my vote for partner.'' Her nose scrunched. 'I don't think Royce counted on that. He thought he had Father in his back pocket. And he did, but not now that Mother and Father understand how much he hurt me.' She laughed. 'Who knows? Maybe connecting with Gillian isn't far behind.'

'Nik, that's wonderful.'

'All four of us have made mistakes. Not only my parents and Gillian, but me too. But my parents are willing to work at being a real family, and so am I.

In fact, Mother felt so bad about pushing Royce on me that she urged Father to pay for my schooling. To make up for not supporting my choices years ago, she said. I want to do this on my own, though, so I told Father I'll apply for a student loan. And no hard feelings.' Her finger skipped down Alex's shirt buttons. 'That's where you come in.'

'Hey, I'm far from rich, but I'll help however I can.'

She grinned. 'I don't need a loan from you, Alex. I need a roommate. The salary at my new job is as pathetic as the one I'm leaving. Rent in Pullman isn't as outrageous as Seattle, but I can't afford a place alone, and my roommates have no plans to leave.'

He gazed at her. Living together was a huge step. He was ready, but was she?

'Is money the only reason you need a roommate?'

'Never.' She kissed him. 'I want a roommate I love, Alex. Preferably someone who loves me, too. And who'll put up with my animals.' A beat passed. 'Do you know anyone?'

Wrapping her in a hug, he kissed her. 'I sure do, Nik. But I'd rather be your husband.' The words tumbled out before he could stop them.

Her eyes twinkled. 'Patience, Dr. Hart. We haven't known each other very long.'

'I don't give a damn. I love you, Nikki, and I want to marry you. I don't care if it happens tomorrow or next year. I can't think of anything that would make me happier.'

'Then the answer's yes. Yes, yes!' She kissed him. An instant later, she pulled away. 'Um, I mean . . . ' She cleared her throat. 'We can discuss marriage another time, after we've lived together awhile.'

He smiled. 'Gun-shy?'

'Just trying to make mature, rational decisions.'

After her experience with Royce, he couldn't blame her. 'Rationalize this.' Tugging her back into his arms, he planted a hot, wet, juicy one on her. As she moaned, he thrust in his tongue. The kiss grew deep and passionate.

'Oooh,' she murmured against his lips. 'Now that's the kind of thing I can rationalize over and over.' A pink flush washed her face. 'I believe I'm in the mood to make a little history with you, professor.' She glanced at the trio. 'As much as I love the fellas, being alone with you sounds incredible.'

'Ask and you shall receive,' Alex replied, having grown fond of folk sayings.

'Then let's make love while the sun shines. Heck, while the moon's shining, too.' She clasped his hand. 'Quick, future fiancé, where's the bedroom?'

Epilogue

Ever After

Lake Eden
May, Eleven Months Later
Nikki yawned and stretched in the queen-sized bed that, three weeks ago, had replaced the two ancient double beds at her cozy lake cabin. Correction: her cabin and Alex's. She no longer thought of the romantic get-away as belonging to her grandparents. They'd passed it down to her; however, over the last year, she and Alex had made the place their own.

Speaking of Alex . . . She glanced at his empty spot in the bed beside her. As promised following their midnight arrival at Lake Eden after enjoying dinner with Karin and her new boyfriend in Seattle, he'd allowed her to sleep in. Lately, work had been kicking her butt. It seemed everyone in Pullman had decided to spay or neuter their cats all at once. Alex was busy, too, teaching Western Civilization and Pacific Northwest History at a small college a short walk from their rented townhouse, with the tiny fenced yard for Bernie and Santos. And Rusty. And their new bunny, Betsy — the only female in their household other than her.

Alex was busy, but not overworked. Axing his obsession about achieving tenure had renewed his enthusiasm for teaching. During his summer break, he planned to continue improvements to the cabin, including repairing the dock and building an eco-friendly, composting outhouse. Then, in the fall, she'd begin vet school at Washington State U.

Nikki wriggled beneath the covers. Who knew that listening to her heart would lead her in the right direction? Toward a career she loved, with the man she loved — Alex Hart, man of her heart, forever and ever.

She couldn't imagine life without him.

Fighting another yawn — they'd made love into the wee hours of morning — she crawled out of bed in her lacy negligee and padded to the bathroom to brush her teeth. The scent of freshly brewed coffee permeated the air, but no animals greeted her. While Alex adored their menagerie as much as she did, a friend at the vet clinic had taken Betsy and the trio for this special weekend.

One year ago today, Nikki had hogtied her handsome professor and spirited him away from his stuffy life. Aside from the miserable weeks they'd suffered apart while each had 'made sure' they loved the other, they'd enjoyed at least a portion of every day together.

Humming as she left the bathroom, she walked across the plank floor she and Alex had painted a cheerful apple green this winter. In the kitchen, she fetched a mug. A note beside the coffeemaker declared, *Happy anniversary, my love*.

Her smile broadened. Twelve months ago, Alex had considered her a nutcase. His sole goal had been to run as fast and far away from her as possible. Now, he still liked to run, but only in the mornings, for exercise before work.

He was probably on his run right now.

She filled her mug. She loved having her coffee at the picnic table in front of the cabin, usually with the dogs nearby while Alex ran. Santos was too old for jogging and Bernie couldn't keep up. She wasn't keen on flashing other lake residents during these brisk May mornings — actually, not at any time — so she retrieved her love's cotton housecoat and tied it over her sexy nightwear. She stuffed bare feet into her grandmother's comfy old slippers and stepped outside with her mug.

As she rounded the path to the picnic table, her gaze drifted along the grassy slope to the lake, glittering in the morning light. At the pebble-strewn shore, a few feet from the dock, a man facing away from her rocked on his heels, hands stuffed in the pants pockets of a superb charcoal suit.

She blinked. *Uh-oh.* She recognized that suit. A few months ago, she'd helped Mr. Fashion Plate pick it out.

'Alex?' Her voice squeaked, little more than a whisper.

He didn't turn.

Heart racing, she repeated louder, 'Alex?'

This time, he turned. A wide smile split his handsome face as he removed his distance glasses and tucked them inside his jacket. When his hand emerged, he held a tiny box.

Nikki's hands flew to her mouth. The mug clattered onto the wood-chip path. By some miracle, the hot coffee didn't soak her slippers.

'Alex Hart, you have a weird sense of timing,' she called. He looked like a movie star, and she hadn't yet showered or done her hair or —

Thank Cupid she'd brushed her teeth!

He laughed. 'Did you get my note?'

Their anniversary! The brilliant man.

She raced across the dewy grass in her cushioned slippers, dodging sharp stones and twigs. Careening to a halt in front of him, she grabbed the box. 'Is this what I think it is?'

He nodded. 'We've waited long enough.'

She popped open the pink velvet ring box. Somewhere in the cobwebby recesses of her mind, a snotty voice lectured that she *should not*, under any circumstances, grab and pop open a ring box. If she practiced a teensy bit of patience, in another moment Alex would drop onto a knee and profess his love.

Screw that.

Breath catching, she gazed at the beautiful peridot-and-diamond ring in an old-fashioned setting — her grandmother's engagement ring. Although Nikki and Gram, both August babies, had shared the light green birthstone, during the annual high-society St. James New Year's bash, Nikki had learned that her mother had inherited the ring. Then — huge shocker — her mom had stored the ring in the safe in her parents' panic room. Like a treasured valuable.

Alex's hands covered hers around the box. 'Your mom gave me the ring in secret in February,' he murmured.

'And you kept it all this time?' Alex and her mother got along famously. Apparently, he appreciated Charlene St. James's wit.

Before he'd entered her life, Nikki hadn't realized her mother possessed a sense of humor, let alone wit.

Then, at Easter, Gillian had yanked the steel rod from her spine long enough to offer Nikki a long, tight sister-hug. They weren't best buds, but they were working on their relationship. Their parents, as well, were focusing on their marriage, including private coun-seling sessions and date nights twice a month.

Nikki and Alex had spent Christmas with his family in Idaho. She adored his parents and sisters, but she'd been going crazy wondering if he'd ever propose again.

'Alex, are you sure?' She looked up from the ring. His hazel eyes shone with love, and her heart pumped like a rapidly inflating balloon. 'Come September, I'll be hitting the books hard. My cooking skills will deteriorate. You'll have to walk Santos and Bernie alone sometimes after your run.'

He shrugged. 'I walk them half the time, anyway, when we can't go together.'

True. Santos followed him everywhere, and Bernie's hyperactivity had decreased to a five out of ten on the Chihuahua scale. Rusty loved kneading Alex's chest at three a.m., which, in Siamese terms, spoke volumes. And Betsy's bunny nose twitched when Alex stroked her soft fur.

Nikki's entire body twitched when he stroked her!

Everyone in her life worshipped the man, including her.

Alex took back the box, removed the ring, and put the box in an outer jacket pocket. Nikki's breath lodged in her lungs as she extended her shaking hand. He clasped it, his palm warm against her fingers. A cool breeze lifted from the lake, and the scents of clean mountain water, spring wildflowers, and blessed nature swirled around them. Alex's housecoat fluttered at her knees.

'Do you remember what you said last year, when I accused you of making love with me on the rebound?' he asked.

Her heart skipped. 'Y-yes.' Something about being of sound mind and —

He slipped the ring onto the tip of her finger, and the thought fled. She couldn't breathe!

'You were right,' he continued. 'You knew what you were doing, and maybe we should have made things official then.'

'Instead of wasting a year.' She

pushed her finger forward — just a little, not too much, surely inconspicuous to the average man — and the ring edged over the base of her fingernail.

Alex nodded. 'But I wouldn't call the last year wasted.'

'Neither would I.' He'd proposed last June, and she, the dimbulb, had suggested waiting.

'Nikki, every moment with you has been a delight, even when we argue.'

'And especially when we make up.'

He chuckled. 'Stop moving your finger.'

'Then get on with it.' She hopped up and down on the pebbled shore.

He gazed into her eyes. 'I want to make up with you for the rest of my life.'

'Alex!'

He drew in a breath. 'Nikki St. James, being of sound mind and a damn horny body, will you marry me?'

Tears crept down her cheeks. He'd remembered her exact words — the romantic fool.

Nodding, she whispered through a tight throat, 'Yes.'

'I love you, Nikki.' He seated the ring onto her finger. A perfect fit.

'I love you, too.' Nikki kissed her fiancé, her forever man. Life was wonderful. Filled with challenges, of course, but they tackled them together. Like her grandparents had. Like Violet and Willie demonstrated every time she and Alex encountered the elderly couple at this special place, Lake Eden. True love's paradise.

They kissed again.

'Alex, I don't want a long engagement,' Nikki said as she relaxed within his embrace. 'Let's have the ceremony in this very spot, with our family and friends. It will be beautiful.' Memorable. Totally them.

He squeezed her waist. 'Excellent idea. Name the date.'

'Mid-July.' Two months away. 'The sun should cooperate. If not, the guests can bring umbrellas.'

'That's my girl, always planning.' His

lips sought out hers again.

During a breathing break, she said, 'I'd like Karin to be my maid of honor.' She hesitated. 'Is that okay?' Her cousin would have performed the duty if Nikki had married . . . that other guy. Neither she nor Alex had seen Royce since the night she'd returned the slime's garish ring. After an unsuccessful confrontation with her father and the other dermatology clinic partners, El Carbuncle had shuffled off to a new life in Pittsburgh.

'Karin's your best friend,' Alex replied. 'I wouldn't have it any other way.'

He really was the most amazing man. 'Who do you want to ask?' To stand up for him. As she'd discovered over the last year, her sexy professor made new friends easily.

'Willie, if he agrees. He knew from the first time he saw us together that we were meant to be.'

'You mean the morning we stopped him — '

' — from whacking Lucy the garter snake to pieces. Yes.'

Nikki beamed. 'I love it. Have you asked him?'

'Not yet. But speak of the devil — '

Hands clasped, they turned. Willie strolled down the slope from two cabins away, shabby jeans encasing his thin legs and chunky boots on his feet. His white T-shirt ruffled against his narrow chest in the brisk morning air.

'Ahoy, young lovers!' The elderly gent waved. 'Vi's fixing blueberry waffles for breakfast. Want to join us?' His arms chugged like pistons at his sides as he neared them. 'Hey, young fellow, what's with the fancy duds?' he asked Alex. His gaze roved over Nikki swaddled in her fiancé's housecoat. A split-second later, eyes snapping to her ring, he whooped. 'I'll be! Took you long enough. When's the weddin'?'

Nikki nudged the man of her heart. Together, they stepped forward.

Alex smiled. 'Funny you should ask . . .'

VALENTINE MASQUERADE

Margaret Sutherland

New Year's Eve is hot and sultry in more ways than one when a tall, handsome prince fixes the newest lady in his court with a magnetic gaze. Who could say no to a prince — especially a charmer like Will Bradshaw? Caitlin has to wonder. And Will wonders, too, if he might have finally found the woman to banish the hurts of years gone by. But what if the one ill-judged mistake of Caitlin's past happens to be the single fault he can't accept?

THE HOUSE ON THE HILL

Miranda Barnes

When a young man moves into the old house next door, Kate Jackson's curiosity is piqued. However, handsome Elek Costas is suspiciously reclusive, and the two get off to a bad start when he accuses her of trespassing. Whilst Kate is dubious of Elek's claim to be the rightful owner, her boyfriend Robert has his eye on acquiring the property for himself . . . Just what is the mystery of Hillside House? Kate is determined to find out!